## ACKNOWLEDGEME

Thank You to my wonderful Husband for your
Without you I would never have been able to

Thank you to my friend, my fan, Jo who proof read for me, even though I suspect she only did it to get an early peak at the second book.

Thank you also to my Friend and fellow author Kate, for your unending help with advice and tips and encouragement.

# HOLLY

I climb out of my car into the cold evening air, shivers wrack my body, but not from the cold. I'm really not looking forward to doing what I came here to do. It's never easy to admit when you were wrong, and it's even harder to apologise for it. I won't be able to rest until I've apologised to Elissa though. I need to do this so I can close this chapter of my life and move on.

Club Entice stands solidly at the back of the car park, lights shining, welcoming people inside. No one would guess just looking at the respectable building what sort of things go on inside. The first time I had come here almost twelve months ago, I had hoped I could find myself inside. Instead I had lost myself, let myself be swayed by someone just to feel like I fit in.

The first few times I had braved going through the door on my own I had stood on the edges of the room feeling awkward and shy. I had made the decision not to bother coming again when Amy had started chatting to me. Feeling relieved that someone was actually talking to me I had ignored my inner voice whispering that she really wasn't a nice person. I'd stood by while she had made people feel bad about themselves, too scared to call her on it in case she turned on me.

The last night I had been in the club she had turned her venom on Elissa and I had stood there while she did. I might not have said anything, but my presence added weight to Amy's words. When Elissa's face had crumpled in front of me I knew I had lost myself totally, I had never been so ashamed of myself, and knowing it had played on Elissa's issues from her past made it all even worse. We could have cost Elissa and Adam their chance to be happy.

My three-month ban is over now though, and the time has come to face my crimes and apologise. Once I had spoken to Elissa and Adam I would walk away from the club and the lifestyle that had tempted me so much. I hadn't found what I was looking for inside the doors of Club Entice anyway.

Taking a deep breath, I walk up to the door and pull it open, warmth and light spill out into the cold night. Stepping into the foyer I am relieved to see it empty apart from Bill behind the desk, maybe I can slip in and out without anyone else noticing me. Bill looks up with his usual cheery smile, but his face hardens when he sees me.

"Well you're braver than Beth, she hasn't dared show her face again." He says sternly.

"I only came back to apologise properly to Elissa and Adam, once I've done that you won't see me again, don't worry." I explain.

"It's a good job they're in then isn't it?" He looks at me and I lower my eyes to escape from his scrutiny.

"Should I just go in, or do you want to check if they want to talk to me?" I hope they will let me speak to them, I don't think I'll have the courage to try again.

"Wait here while I get someone to cover the desk and I'll take you in myself." He disappears through the club door.

This was so much worse than I thought it would be, but after the way I had behaved what more could I expect? He's gone so long I begin to think he's forgotten about me, or maybe they don't want to talk to me and he's hoping I'll just leave. I turn to do just that and I'm almost at the door when I hear the club door open behind me.

"Lost your nerve then?" Bill's harsh voice halts my progress across the thick black carpet.

"No, not at all. I thought you had changed your mind about letting me in." I turn back to face him.

"Oh no, if anyone deserves an apology it's Elissa, you owe her that much." He pulls the door open and waves me through in front of him.

The club is full as usual for a Friday, and several people frown when they see me. It shouldn't surprise me, I knew it was going to be bad when I had decided to come back. I didn't expect anyone to welcome me back, I didn't deserve it.

Bill grabs my arm and leads me around the dance floor to a quieter seating area towards the back of the club. My steps falter when I see the four people sat waiting for me, Leo and Gemma with Adam and Elissa. The two men have the same stern look on their faces that Bill has, I feel my body begin to shake and my hands are sweating. I just need to take a deep breath and get this over with, then I can leave.

As we get closer to the seating area I risk a look at Elissa, she's sitting with her head held high and her hand held tight by Adam. I'm so glad to see that Amy didn't manage to chase Elissa away like she wanted to. Bill pushes me forward until I'm just a few steps away from Elissa.

"Get on with it then girly." He says with a nudge to my back.

"Will you three stop it, you're scaring the poor girl to death." I'm shocked to hear the words coming from Elissa.

"Little mouse, she's one of the people who hurt you and made you leave, she doesn't deserve your notice." Adam says gently, pulling her closer to him.

"Sir, Amy was the one who hurt me, Holly just wasn't brave enough to stand up to her, I wouldn't have been either." I gasp in shock.

Could this woman really be defending me? I look at her in confusion and she gives me a gentle smile.

"Sir, can I speak to Holly alone for a few minutes please?"

"No Elissa, I won't leave you alone with her." He sounds angry and I take half a step back.

"Then leave Gemma with me, but I need you and Leo to leave us to talk without the two of you glaring at her like that." She looks pleadingly at him.

"Okay, if you're sure." He stands and takes a step closer to me. "I'm still watching you, if she looks upset in any way I will have Bill throw you out. Do you understand?"

"Yes, I understand." I whisper.

The three men walk away to the next seating area, but I can still feel them glaring at me.

"Sit down Holly, I'm so sorry about Adam, he's still feeling very protective when it comes to me." She smiles at me and pats the seat next to her.

I sit and risk a glance in Gemma's direction, she wasn't glaring, but she didn't look exactly welcoming either.

"He's entitled to feel protective after what happened, especially when it comes to me."

"You're very brave to come back Holly." She says gently.

"I'm sorry I'm making you think about that night again, I've only come back in to apologise to you in person, I won't be back after tonight." I explain.

"Amy is the person who should be saying sorry." Gemma chips in.

"Well I won't hold my breath for that." Elissa laughs.

"I'm so so sorry, I should have walked away when I realised what she was like. I definitely shouldn't have stood by and let her do what she did to you."

"Why did you?" Gemma asks sharply.

"When I first came in here no one spoke to me, I was too shy to talk to anyone, it's hard coming somewhere like this alone. Amy asked me to join her for a drink and I thought she was a friend, by the time I realised what she was like, I was too scared of her to say anything. I should have just stopped coming to the club, that would have been the best way."

"Why did you come to the club in the first place?" Elissa asks.

"I was interested in the lifestyle, I read a few books and thought I should come along and see if I could find what I had read about, but I didn't." I reply sadly.

"Do you still want to find it? Are you still interested?"

"I am, but I don't think I'll find it, I don't think it's out there for me."

"Well it won't be if you stop coming in the club." Gemma says with a roll of her eyes.

"I can't do it anymore, I don't fit in here. I just wanted to say how incredibly sorry I am for what happened, and I'm so glad you didn't let Amy scare you away."

"Apology accepted Holly." Elissa says, gently patting my hand.

"Thank you, it's more than I deserve. I'm really glad you found your happiness." I get up from the seat and walk back towards the door.

## BILL

I watch as Holly straightens her back and turns to walk out of the club. She looks so sad, like she's lost something important. She's standing tall against the disapproval flowing towards her in waves from the rest of the club though. I like that, she did something wrong, yes, but she was brave enough to admit that and come and deliver her apology.

"So, she really did just come in to apologise then." Leo says.

"Seems so, I'm just glad she didn't upset Elissa again. Hopefully that's the end of it all." Adam walks back to Elissa and pulls her into his arms.

"That was hard for Adam to do, leave Elissa alone with Holly, he hasn't forgotten how hurt she was." Leo's gaze follows Holly as she walks towards the door.

"Well none of us like seeing someone we care for hurt." I reply.

"No, we don't, and that's one hurt woman walking out the door right there." He nods in Holly's direction.

"What do you mean? She's the one who hurt Elissa."

"Amy is the one who hurt Elissa, Holly was just too scared to stand against her. I think Amy used to pick people who felt alone, I think she knew that they wanted to fit in and made them feel like they did. The question is, why did Holly feel like she needed to so much that she let her relief overcome her better judgement?" He turns and walks over to Gemma, his wife.

Leo might be a quiet man, but he didn't miss much, if he said Holly hadn't felt like she fit in, then I had missed something and I needed to make it right. I follow her to the door and catch up with her just as she walks out into the foyer.

"Wait just a minute Holly." She turns back to face me and there are tears rolling down her cheeks.

"I apologised, that's all I wanted to do. Don't worry, I won't be back." She turns to leave and I catch her wrist halting her progress.

"Let's have a little chat before you leave. If you still want to leave after that, then I won't stop you." I gesture to the chair at the side of my desk and she reluctantly sits in it.

"what do you want to talk about? I've said I'm sorry for what I did." She asks confused.

"That's not what I want to talk to you about." She looks up at me, obviously wondering what else I could possibly want to talk to her about.

"Why did you start coming to the club?"

"I was interested in exploring the lifestyle. I thought it might be what I was looking for."

"Do you still think it might be?" I ask.

"No, I didn't find it in the couple of scenes I've had. I don't think what I'm looking for exists for me."

"What is it you are looking for?"

"Well that's the problem, I'm not exactly sure, I just know I haven't found it yet. I thought it might be the scene, but the two scenes I had just didn't feel right, didn't feel like I had imagined they would." She shrugs.

"So, how did you expect a scene to feel?"

"It doesn't matter, it didn't feel that way anyway."

"Answer my question girly." I snap and she jerks in response.

"I thought it would take me away from myself, take me to a world of feeling through the pain and the submission." A very interesting answer.

"You're a masochist?"

"I don't know, the idea of pain excites me, I wanted to know what it would feel like to be carried away on a wave of pain." Her voice is almost wistful.

"Do you still want to know?"

"It doesn't matter now, I can't come back to the club."

"Why not? Your ban is over, there's no reason why you can't." I explain.

"No, it took all my courage to come in here on my own in the first place, and look where it got me."

"What if you weren't alone?"

Something about this woman has captured my interest, not least because it seems she might share my love of pain. Of course, I loved delivering the pain, not experiencing it. I hadn't found anyone with whom I could give my sadistic side free reign in a long time, so long people seemed to have forgotten it was there, hidden behind the smiling face.

"I don't understand" she says confused.

"Let me ask you another question?" I ask "The two scenes you had before. What word would you use to describe them?"

"They were nice, I suppose." She whispers.

"Nice should never be the word you use to describe something intense." She obviously hadn't clicked with whoever she scened with.

"That's the thing, they weren't that intense. They were okay, just not what I thought it would be."

"Do you still want to know what it feels like? To be swept away by something so intense that you forget who you are?" I could show her, something tells me we would click.

"It doesn't matter." She stands and moves to walk to the door.

"STOP!" I snap and she freezes automatically.

"Sir?" She turns and looks questioningly at me.

"I asked you a question, and I expect an answer. Do you still want to know what it feels like?"

"Yes." The word comes out on an excited breath.

"Then let me show you, at least then you will know exactly what you are turning your back on."

## Holly

Oh my, was he actually saying he would scene with me? Why would he do that? I'd seen the look on his face when I came in. His scowl said it all, he was always so cheerful and jokey, the fact he showed his anger told me exactly what he thought of me.

"Why would you want to? Is this so you can punish me some more?"

"No Holly, you served your ban and you came back to apologise, that's the end of it as far as I'm concerned."

"Then why?"

"I missed something going on in my club, I slipped up, if I had known you were finding it hard fitting in I would have introduced you to people. Maybe then Amy wouldn't have got her claws in you."

"That's not your fault, nor your responsibility." I argue.

"I don't want you to walk away from something just because you haven't found the right person to show you."

"Ah, so it's show and tell? Don't bother, I'm not a pity case." I turn towards the door again and he lets me grab hold of the handle before he speaks.

"Be here at eight next Friday, if you still want to know I will show you. If not, you will always wonder." His words follow me out into the freezing air of the carpark.

His words follow me through my day and creep into my sleep for the next few days, whispering in my ear. Annoyingly he was right, I would always wonder what it would have felt like if I'd been brave enough to try one last time. Should I go back? I had already been doubting what I was looking for actually existed outside of erotic fiction. It all sounded good in the books on my kindle, but was that all it was? Did people actually feel that swept away in real life?

On Thursday night I lie awake in bed for the third night in a row wondering what to do. I was going to be fit for nothing at work tomorrow, not that my job in the call centre needed much attention. It wouldn't do to fall asleep on the job though, no matter how boring it was. I need to decide if I'm going to go back to the club tomorrow or not, so I can put it out of my mind and finally sleep.

Bill had always been so nice and cheerful, especially when he was on the front desk, I had only seen him play with someone once or twice though. His scenes always looked fun, he laughed a lot and didn't seem to take himself too seriously, lots of Dom types seemed to think they would lose all credibility if they cracked a smile. Could he really have a sadistic side? I'd never seen any hint of it before.

He seemed to think he could give me the scene I had imagined, surely, I owe it to myself to give it a try. If this one doesn't work though I am definitely done with the whole idea. Decision made I finally fall asleep, it's not a restful sleep though, it's disturbed by dreams of canes and floggers.

When my alarm goes off it feels as though I've only been asleep for a few minutes. Today was going to be a long work day. By the time I finish work for the day and head to my car I'm a curious mixture of bone weary tired and strung tight anticipation.

Eating is impossible I'm too nervous, so I jump in the shower as soon as I get home. Maybe I can force something down later. I shampoo my hair while mentally reviewing my wardrobe, my red skirt and corset would be good for tonight, I may as well go out with a bit of flare.

Would anyone even speak to me tonight? Probably not if last week was anything to go by, at least Elissa had accepted my apology. It's just one more night, an experiment not a social evening. I could get through one more night, just to put the idea to rest once and for all.

The car park is already full when I get to the club, oh joy, more people to witness my last night. The lights filtering through the windows of the entrance fill the car park with a warm glow and the Club Entice logo over the door calls to me. Would I finally find the type of scene I had read about? Or was tonight just going to be another disappointment? Pulling the door open I step inside to find out.

# BILL

Looking up as the door opens again I see Holly, I really hadn't been sure she would come back. She looks amazing, the red skirt swirls around her legs and the red satin corset has done spectacular things to her waist and cleavage. She looks nervous, was it because of our promised scene or just because she was back in the club?

She walks slowly up to the desk and her eyes automatically lower as she stops in front of me.

"Stand to one side girly, I will be with you as soon as I get the desk covered." I hear her slight gasp.

Obviously, she hadn't expected the scene to begin right away. It suited my purpose to have her slightly on edge. If the two Dom's she had already scened with hadn't managed to take her control away tonight would come as a shock.

I ring through to the club room, to ask someone to come and cover the desk, I can see her fidgeting as she waits. I was going to enjoy myself tonight, whether she will enjoy it is another matter. One of the bar staff comes through from the club room to cover the desk for me, as he gets to the desk and see's Holly waiting he makes a disapproving noise.

I see her flinch as she hears the same disapproval. She keeps her eyes lowered and stands still as instructed though. I walk over to her and lift her chin, tears are glistening in her eyes and hurt fills her face.

"Breath deeply Holly, you are here at my invitation, anyone who has a problem with that can take it up with me."

I hear a noise from behind the desk.

"Do you have a problem Jason?" I snap.

"She doesn't belong here after what she did. No one wants her here, especially Adam and Elissa."

Holly stiffens at the harsh words, but she doesn't look surprised.

"Don't speak for me Jason, I am perfectly capable of speaking for myself." Elissa's voice comes from the doorway behind us. "Holly has apologised for being manipulated by Amy and I have accepted her apology, she is welcome here anytime as far as I'm concerned."

"I won't have any ill feeling in my club Jason, so you better adjust your attitude." I turn my sternest look on Jason and he automatically takes a step back, then flushes as he realises how much that step told me.

I turn back to Holly and see she is trembling.

"I should leave." She whispers.

"No, you should stand tall and stay, you paid your penance for what you did, you apologised and accepted responsibility. The lifestyle we lead follows certain rules, one of which is that once a punishment and apology has been completed that's an end to the matter."

"I don't want to cause trouble."

"The only people who will cause trouble are people who don't mind their own business, and keep their opinions to themselves. Anyone who gives you any trouble will be guilty of the same behaviour Amy showed to Elissa and will suffer the same consequence's."

Jason looks shocked at my statement. The behaviour is the same though, it's all a form of bullying and I won't have it in my club.

"Okay, lets go into the club room." I nudge her in the direction of the door. "Get moving girly."

She quickens her pace and pulls open the door, lowering her gaze and waiting for me to enter before her. She obviously wants to hide behind me as long as possible. Well that wasn't happening.

"Go in front of me Holly." She looks at me with pleading eyes, but seeing my face she sighs and walks through the door into the busy room.

I lead her through the room to the seating area near the back, when she moves to kneel on the floor I shake my head and gesture to the sofa at the side of me.

"Time for a chat I think Holly, we need to find out what you like and don't like."

"I don't really know." She whispers.

"Well let's start with hard limits shall we, you must know what your hard limits are."

"Yes, I have hard limits. I won't be gagged." She shudders at the thought.

"I can live without gagging you, any more?"

"I don't want any permanent marks left on my skin."

"I never leave permanent marks, there will be marks though, bruises and stripes, is that a problem?"

"No, that's fine. I won't do any play involving pee or scat." Again, with the shudder of dislike.

"That's not something I've ever been tempted to try so don't worry about that. Any soft limits I need to know about?"

"I don't like my feet being touched, especially tickled."

"But it's not a hard limit?"

"No, I just don't like it. Other than that, I don't really know, I haven't tried that much yet."

"Okay, well I think we can work with most of that. Now, what about this fascination with pain you seem to have? Do you want to explore pain and what it can do for you?"

I watch her face as the flush rushes up from her chest, turning her cheeks pink with excitement and arousal. Her pupils dilate and her breathing speeds up. Definitely interested in exploring pain, well I could help her with that. Hopefully I could give her the type of scene she had been imagining and in the process, stop her from running away from the lifestyle.

"Kneel for me now girly." I point at the floor next to my feet and she immediately slides off the sofa onto her knees.

"Good girl, now be good and wait until I decide it's time to play."

"Yes Sir." She says sweetly.

I look up to see Adam approaching with Elissa just behind him. He inclines his head in question and I nod and gesture for him to sit.

"Kneel next to Holly little mouse." He commands Elissa and she gracefully sinks to the floor next to a shaking Holly. I see her hand reach out to pat Holly's shaking fingers, compassionate sub, how generous of her to comfort the person who had been involved in the nasty little scene that had hurt her so badly.

"Adam, how are you?" He looks so relaxed and happy, they really are happy together.

"I'm good Bill, how are you?"

"I'm okay, anticipating exploring a little with Holly later, she's interested in pain."

"Really? That's surprising, she doesn't strike me as a masochist, and it's a long time since I've seen that sadistic gleam in your eye." He laughs.

"I know, I think people have forgotten its there at all."

"Well you haven't let that side of you out to play for a long time, are you still up to it?"

"Cheeky bugger, watch and learn, just watch and learn." Standing, I hold my hand out to a trembling Holly. "Time to play girly, up you get."

"Yes Sir." She puts her hand in mine, and with it hands over her control to me.

# HOLLY

What am I doing? I can't believe I'm actually here about to scene with Bill. He has always seemed so easy going on the front desk, but listening to him talking to Adam, I'm beginning to wonder. I don't know where my fascination with pain comes from, I've never thought of myself as having a high pain threshold. When I have read erotic fiction though I am always swept away by the description of masochists and their love of pain.

Well, I was about to find out what it's like to be swept away by sensation, hopefully anyway. I follow Bill over to the St Andrews cross near the centre of the room. He pulls the reserved sign off the cross and opens his toy bag. He pulls out a set of cuffs and looks at me. Pulling in a deep breath, I take the last step closer and hold my wrists out to him.

"Good girl." He says and buckles the cuffs on my wrists, checking to make sure they aren't too tight.

He pulls me forward and clips my wrists to the upper hooks on the cross, stretching my arms high above my head. My body is taught and stretched, my breasts peaking over the top of my corset, it feels sexy and decadent. He steps closer to me and his hands come around my ribs to the corset fastening, he yanks it open and I feel my breasts spill out. Next my skirt is yanked down and my thong is ripped off. He hasn't said a word, just ruthlessly stripped me naked.

"What is your safe word Holly?" He whispers in my ear.

"Red, it's easy to remember."

"You may use it if you need to, other wise the only words I want to hear from you are yes Sir."

I nod in agreement.

"Let me hear the words girly." He snaps.

"Yes Sir." This was nothing like the two scenes I had before, I feel on edge and nervous, Bill was an unknown entity to me, he seemed so cold.

"Good girl, now, lets see if I can show you what you have been dreaming about."

Oh God, this was it, can I take the amount of pain I think I'm about to get? I shiver as a panic starts to creep in, I had dreamt about the sensation of pain, but this would be the first time I've ever tried it. I don't know if I can do this, could I call red before we even start?

"Are you still with me Holly? What's going on in that head?" His warm hands stroke over my shoulders, bringing me back to the room and what's about to happen.

"I'm a bit scared Sir." I need to be honest with him.

"You wouldn't be human if you weren't, this is the first time we have played and I intend to take you further into the feeling of pain than you have been before. Trust me to keep you safe, but show you what you need."

I pull in a deep breath and try to relax my body, I know impact hurts a lot more if the body is tense. Letting my breath out in a big gush, my body relaxes against the cross and my mind calms. I can hear him moving about behind me and the longer I wait the bigger the feeling of submission gets.

The first blow of the paddle takes my breath away, I hadn't realised he had finished getting ready. He paddles both cheeks in a hard rhythm, each whack sends a rush of stinging sensation over my body. Just when it begins to be too much, he pauses and runs his hands over my hot skin, making me gasp again.

His foot pushes my legs further apart and I feel air brush over my damp folds. How am I so wet so quickly? His fingers trail down to brush over my pussy lips and I hear him chuckle behind me.

"Oh, you do like pain don't you girly?" His fingers tease my entrance and a small groan escapes.

"Let's see how much pain you like." He steps away and I feel the cool air of the room against my back.

I feel the falls of a flogger trail across my back, the ends tickling the hot skin of my bottom. I do enjoy the feeling of a flogger.

Wham! A heavy paddle lands on my left cheek and I yelp in surprise. I'd thought he was going to hit me with the flogger, but he must have a paddle in his other hand. Again, I hear him laugh behind me, he really was a sadistic bastard.

The flogger lands with a sharp sting on the abused flesh of my arse and I arch into the pain. It feels so good, so overwhelming. My mind was still firmly in the room though, no sweeping away yet. Maybe I was reaching for something that just doesn't exist.

"You seem to be thinking a lot over there girly. I think you need a bit more pain to let go."

The flogger lands hard on my other cheek and just before the feeling fades the wham of the paddle hits the same spot. A rush of sensation sweeps over me and I grab hold of the chains holding my wrists. He uses the flogger over and over and just when I least expect it the paddle lands with a harsh slap. The skin of my arse feels on fire and I'm gasping for breath, he steps close behind me and the rough denim of his jeans brushes against my heated flesh, making me gasp again.

"I think you are nicely warmed up now, don't you? Time to get down to business."

Oh my God, this was his idea of a warm up? The two Dom's I had scened with before hadn't taken me this far in the whole scene, let alone a warm up.

Something cool brushes against my nipples and I look down to see a riding crop, this was going to hurt. He teases my nipples with the crop until I whimper in frustration. Then he pulls it back and brings it down hard on the outside of my left breast, the sting is intense and I look in wonder as the red welt springs up on my skin.

Fingers brush against my pussy and I can feel how wet I am. My clit is beginning to throb with need and I feel my arousal coating my thighs. Pain really does turn me on. His fingers continue playing with me as the crop lands against my breast again. I groan and arch up onto my tip toes, clinging to the chains to stop myself sagging.

He uses the riding crop on my right breast and then brings it down on the cheeks of my arse in a relentless pattern. My mind is filled with stinging pleasure pain and I can feel my grip on reality begin to fade.

He pinches the tender flesh of my bottom and twists the abused flesh, making me yelp again with shock at the overwhelming sting.

"Open your eyes Holly, look at me." His voice drifts through the sensation fogging my brain and I struggle to obey. I manage to lift my heavy lids and Bill's face fills my vision.

He smiles and I can't help but smile back.

"There you are." He grips the back of my head and takes my lips in a brutal kiss. I whimper and my knees buckle with the onslaught of feeling.

"Are you ready for my cane now?" He asks.

"Yes Sir." I just want this feeling to last forever.

He steps back again and I wait, anticipating the sting of the cane against my hot flesh. The first stroke of the cane flames across both cheeks of my arse, lifting me onto my toes and stealing my breath.

"Yes, you like that don't you girly?" I groan in response.

The cane lands in even measured strokes up and down my arse, each stroke sends stinging sensation bursting through my body, the sensation reaches my brain and then rushes back down to my clit, arousing me even more.

He continues to use the cane in a deliberate rhythm over my arse, then suddenly he brings the cane down where my arse meets my thigh. My brain shuts down and I hear a high-pitched scream coming from deep inside. Something cracks open inside me and all the feeling rushes in to fill the space left behind.

As the stinging blows continue I am carried away on a tide of sensation, it's as though my body and mind are saying finally!

## BILL

I can't remember when I last enjoyed a scene this much. She definitely was a masochist, she was totally gone, deep into subspace. The connection between us during the scene had been electric. To watch her give in to the pain and sensation had been such a gift, for her to trust me enough to send her to subspace was a very precious gift indeed.

Stepping in close to her again I run my fingers through the slick wetness between her thighs. A low deep groan of pleasure is her response to the extra sensation. Her back arches, pushing her hot red arse against my uncomfortable hard on. The friction from my jeans against her sensitive flesh pushes her up on her toes.

"Open your eyes girly." She shakes her head, not really hearing me.

I grab a handful of her hair and yank her head back.

"Holly, open your eyes and look at me." I snap.

Her eyes open slowly as though they are held down by weights, she sighs in contentment, she is totally lost in a world of sensation and pain. I look into her eyes to gauge her reaction as I brush my finger over her clit. Her head falls back in total surrender, she has given herself to me, such an act of submission deserves a reward.

I push two fingers deep into her pussy and rub my thumb over her clit. She tries to move against my hand to increase the friction and I slap her arse. She gasps as the shock of the slap rushes over her, I thrust my fingers in and out of her sopping pussy, stretching the sensation of the slap out with the added sensation of arousal.

She was mine to play with and torment, her mind was free and her body relaxed, the connection between us increased with every minute we played. I've reached the place where I can sense every movement of her body and every sensation she is feeling.

Now was the time to take us both further on this journey, pushing us both deeper into the scene and increasing the connection between us.

I pinch her nipple hard as I rub my fingers against her G-spot and my thumb across her clit. She lets out a high whine of pleasure and I squeeze her nipple tighter. Her eyes are glazed and her skin is covered with a fine layer of sweat. She's primed and ready for me to push her that little bit further over the edge into the release of orgasm.

I press down hard on her clit and squeeze on her nipple hard, that's all it takes. Her high scream of release echo's around the club and several people stop to watch. She sags against the cross and I pull her close to me with my arm around her waist. Reaching up I release the cuffs from the chains and pick her up as she falls against me.

Grabbing a blanket from the shelf to one side of the cross I carry her over to the sofa. Holding her close on my knee I wrap her from neck to toe in the warm fleece of the blanket. Her sigh of contentment brushes over my neck and I relax back against the sofa, my own feeling of contentment washes over me. I hadn't let my sadistic side out for a long time, too long.

Maybe Holly was the person I could finally play with the way I want to. The last sub I had played this hard with had been my partner, my girlfriend. We had been in a relationship for four years and I had thought we had a good thing going. That was until I had found out she had been cheating on me for six months with another member of the club.

I haven't really played with anyone seriously in the two years since. This bundle of submissive masochist I held in my arms had given me back a huge part of myself. I just hope I have helped her find what she had been searching for when she had come into the club. Hopefully I had shown her that this lifestyle could give her the feelings she needs, not just the upset and hurt that Amy had shown her.

Looking down into her face, all I see is relaxed contentment, no lines of tension or pain mar her pretty face. I want to explore S/m more with her, I really want to see how she reacts to pain mixed with sex. Would she give us the chance to explore deeper together?

I look up from the little sub in my arms to see Adam watching me from the other sofa, a huge grin on his face. Elissa is looking slightly horrified, for a sub like her our scene must have looked brutal. Elissa had only been introduced to the scene six months ago by Adam and she definitely wasn't into serious pain.

Adam leans forward and whispers in her ear, I don't know what he says, but her shoulders relax and she gives me a timid smile. Not many people have seen this side of me, most have only seen the jolly smiling Bill as they sign in at the front desk. Long term members of the club, like Adam and Leo will remember this side of me though.

It's time to let this part of me out to play again, I'd kept it closed away too long. There needed to be so much trust between two people to really indulge in S/m, a trust I hadn't felt able to give someone since I'd found out Hannah was cheating.

It was past time to let that go, I had been holding onto her betrayal, using it to keep people from getting too close. It was a very lonely way to live, and I'm tired of being lonely.

Holly was a very comfortable arm full, that's for sure. Her blonde hair is sticking to her sweat sheened face, her eyes are still closed, but her breathing has slowed and her pulse has returned to normal. Her body is relaxed against my chest and her breath flutters against my neck, teasing and keeping my cock hard. I can still feel the adrenaline flowing through my body, the high from the scene will take a while to wear off.

Top space is something I don't achieve very often and it was always special when it happens.

# HOLLY

I'm drifting in a warm soft cloud, I want to stay here forever. Voices are beginning to invade my peace though, intruding on my silent contentment. I snuggle further into the warm softness and as I do I become aware that I'm being held tight against a hard chest by strong arms. I know it's a hard chest, because I can hear the steady heart beat against my ear. It's comforting and I try to focus on it and block out the voices.

Something warm brushes my face and I instinctively turn towards the warmth.

"Are you coming back to me girly?" The question is whispered against my ear. The voice is gentle and reminds me of someone, but I don't have any desire to remember who.

I don't need to know, I just need to enjoy my warm cloud.

"Not quite yet, it seems." The same voice, then a laugh.

Something in the voice is pulling me towards it, it speaks of safety, and the temptation of belonging. I need to pull myself towards the voice, to leave my cloud and return to him. I try to open my eyes, but it feels like there are weights holding them closed. I focus on getting my eyes to open, it seems to take much more concentration than I feel it should.

Finally, I open my eyes and look up into Bill's face. He's smiling down at me, the happy, laughing Dom once more. The Sadist and the happy Dominant, two sides to one man.

"Hello." I whisper. "Thank you." He had shown me that what I was looking for did actually exist.

"There you are girly, welcome back." He smiles gently at me.

"Thank you."

"You already said that, what are you thanking me for?" He asks gently.

"For showing me it's really out there." At least now I know, although it's going to make it harder to walk away from.

"Well now, you are very welcome. Thank you for trusting me enough to let me show you." He hands me a bottle of water and I take a refreshing mouthful.

"I should go." I move to stand up and his arm clamps me to his side.

"Where do you think you are going?" His voice snaps

"Home."

"I don't think so girly." I struggle against his hold. "Keep still girl." He snaps and I instinctively freeze in his hold.

"Let me go." I plead.

"No, you have just spent fifteen minutes in subspace after an intense scene, no way are you driving home until I decide you are safe to do so."

I suppose he has a point, I do still feel quite out of it.

"Okay, but at least let me go and freshen up and put some clothes on."

"I think you are forgetting your place girly, remember where you are." His face turns stern and hard.

Oh no, I had forgotten where I was, I knew how to behave in the club.

"I'm sorry Sir." I whisper lowering my head to escape his gaze.

"That's better, now stay put until I think you are recovered enough to move."

I settle back against his chest, if I have to stay here for a few minutes I might as well make the most of it. I let my gaze wonder around the room and see Elissa kneeling at Adams feet across from us. She is looking at me with concern, this woman who should hate me, is concerned for me. The intense feeling of shame that rushes in makes me gasp, I should leave now and never come back.

"What was that thought girly?"

"Please let me go, I shouldn't be here." I struggle to get out of his hold and escape.

"Look at me." He lifts my chin to look into my eyes.

"I'm sorry, I should leave." I whisper.

"Why do you think you don't belong here?"

"Because I did a horrible thing, I hurt Elissa, people don't want me here, everyone would be happier if I left."

"Yes, you did hurt Elissa, that's true, but you are sorry and you said you were sorry, Elissa accepted your apology, she has forgiven you, but clearly you haven't forgiven yourself. "

"I'm so ashamed of what I did, I know Amy did it, but I had a choice, I could have left, well I'm stronger now, I can leave now."

"You know, you're going to give me a complex, all this talk of running away." He says with a laugh.

"I'm not running away, I said I would come back for one night so you could show me, well now you've shown me and I know. Now I can leave and forget all about this club and what I did."

"I don't think you can forget Holly. I think this is a part of who you are. You can't turn your back on yourself and you can never escape from yourself."

"I can't carry on coming in here on my own, it's too hard, I don't belong, Amy showed me that."

"Does Club Entice belong to Amy? I must have missed the memo from the previous owner."

"No one wants me here." Now didn't that sound pathetic.

"Well now girly, that's where you are wrong. I think I for one will quite like having you around."

"Me too." Elissa says from her spot on the floor.

I look across to see her smiling at me.

"Little mouse, didn't I teach you better than that? You know you shouldn't interrupt anyone's scene or aftercare." Adam yanks her head back with her hair.

"I'm sorry Sir." She doesn't look sorry.

"I'm not the one you need to be saying sorry to, am I?" He nods towards Bill.

A fearful look crosses her face, surely, she wasn't afraid of Bill, he was always so nice.

"Now don't look at me like that, you'll make me feel bad." Bill laughs.

"I'm sorry Bill, I think your sadistic side scared her a bit." Adam smiles. "Apologise to Bill pet."

"I'm sorry for interrupting." Elissa looks down at the floor.

"Apology accepted, especially since you were helping prove my point." Bill smiles.

He turns and pins me with his stare.

"People do want you here, you do belong in this club as long as I say you do, now go and get dressed and join me at the front desk, we need to talk about our scene." He pushes me up onto my wobbling legs.

Perhaps he was right, maybe I do need to recover for a little while before I drive home.

# BILL

I watch as she stumbles off to the changing room, trailing her blanket behind her.

"Would you like Elissa to go and make sure she's okay?" Adam asks

I turn to see a smug knowing look on his face.

"Elissa, I would be grateful if you could check on Holly, it was an intense scene and her first subspace."

"Go ahead little mouse." Elissa gets to her feet and heads to the locker room.

"Go on then, get it over with." I turn back to Adam, waiting for the ribbing I know he's dying to dish out.

"I'm not going to say anything, except, it's about bloody time."

"What's that supposed to mean?"

"Its about time you moved on, I know Hannah hurt you, but you've held onto it for far too long."

"I know, it's time to move on."

"With Holly?"

"I don't know, but the potential is there. Now keep your nose out."

I walk away with the sound of his laugh in my ears.

Back at the reception desk I dismiss a sheepish Jason and sit to wait for Holly. It should be quiet out here now; most people are already inside. I love the ebb and flow of club nights, the vibe and atmosphere of so many people being free to play how they like is intoxicating.

I love my job, not many people can say that, but I truly enjoy every minute I'm here. I really enjoyed showing Holly what a real scene can be like. She had slipped into sub space so easily, carried away by the pain and sensation. A true masochist, for a true Sadist to enjoy. Not if she didn't come back to the club though.

The club room door opens and she's stood there looking all shy and embarrassed.

"Come and sit while we talk Holly."

"I should go home." She says hesitantly moving towards the door.

"Sit down girly." I snap and she automatically drops into the chair.

She looks at me with trepidation, obviously wondering what I'm going talk about.

"How are you feeling?" I ask gently.

"I'm okay Sir." An automatic reply from someone who is uncomfortable talking about their feelings.

"Do you still feel spacy?"

"Not so much now." She does still have a floaty look in her eye.

"How did the scene make you feel? Did you find what you were looking for?" I remind her that she had been looking for this.

"Oh, it was wonderful, being swept away like that was amazing, like nothing I've ever felt before." Her whole face lights up with joy.

"So why are you in such a rush to leave?" I ask.

"I don't belong here. I can't keep coming in here on my own, it's too hard. Thank you though for showing me this one time, for letting me see what it's really like."

"Don't you want to explore this further?" I can't let her just walk away.

"Part of me does, but…." She lets the words trail off.

"But what" I push.

"Why does it matter to you?" She looks at me with curious eyes.

"It matters because you aren't the only one searching for something, and I think we might have what each other needs."

## HOLLY

A picture fills my head at his words. A picture of me and Bill together in the club, exploring the limits of pain together. I had promised myself this one last night though, now he was making me long for more.

"Why would you want me to keep coming back?" I ask, he must have a reason, it wasn't like he ever lacked play partners.

"Because for the first time in too long you gave my Sadist the chance to come out and play." He smiles.

"You play every week though, you're never short of someone willing to scene with you." I'm confused.

"Yes, I scene with others, but none of them are masochists, you, girly are definitely a masochist." There is a wicked gleam in his eye.

"So, it's just because I can take the pain you dish out?"

"No, lots of women can take the pain, it's because you enjoy feeling the pain just as much as I enjoy giving the pain, you get off on it."

"So basically, you just want me to keep coming into the club so you can scratch your Sadistic itch when you feel like it?" That didn't sound fun for me.

"No that's not what I'm suggesting at all." He sounds insulted.

"What exactly are you suggesting then?"

"I'm suggesting that we explore together, exclusively. I think we could both find something good and rewarding, together."

Was he actually suggesting a relationship?

"Just in the club?" I need to make sure exactly what he is suggesting.

"To begin with yes, but things may develop further, you never know."

"So, you would be my Sir?"

"Yes, you would be my submissive, you would only play with me." He looks intently into my eyes.

"Why? Is this just because you feel sorry for me, am I a pity case now?"

"No, this is because I see something in you that speaks to something in me."

"I don't know what to say. Can I think about it for a while?" I don't want to make a decision while I'm still feeling the effects of our play.

"You can give me your answer next Friday when you come back."

"I haven't said I'm coming back yet."

"No, but you will. Now you've had a taste of what I can give you nothing will stop you." Cocky man.

"I still feel I should stay away."

"Holly, why are you trying so hard to deny who you are? Just let yourself be, you can't change the core of who you are. You can try and supress it, but it will just eat you up from inside and ruin every relationship you try to have." He grips the back of my neck to emphasise his point.

"I don't like who I became when I was here before, what I did was wrong, it's not who I am. This place made me try too hard to fit in and I ended up hurting someone because of it."

"I'll give you a bit of advice to think on, stop trying to fit in. The only thing you need to be is yourself."

Stop trying to fit in? His words rock me to the core, if I didn't need to fit in I could just enjoy the club and watching the play without the pressure. I'd spent so much energy trying to fit in and I'd never felt like I managed it. If I just stopped trying would I be happier?

"Now, you need to go home and get some rest, think long and hard about what I've said and I will see you here next Friday with an answer, even if it's a no." His tone leaves no room to argue.

"Yes Sir." I stand up and turn to leave.

"Oh, and girly, enjoy your tender arse over the next couple of days." With his words he delivers a sharp crack of his hand to my sore hot bottom.

I yelp in surprise and his laughter follows me out to the car park.

As I lie in bed later, I think back over what had happened tonight. The sensations had been overwhelming, they had literally shut my mind off. I still don't know how long I had been out of it.

So, all my books were right, it was out there, this feeling of being swept away by someone else. Not just by him though, by the pain too. The sting of the pain had rushed over me like a wild fire, burning along my nerves and leaving a feeling of being washed clean.

Could I turn my back on it, pretend it didn't exist? It was everything I had been searching for when I had gone to the club in the first place. Bill had given me a true gift. What would he do if I didn't go on Friday? Not much probably, he doesn't even know where I live.

On the other hand, though, what if I did go back and explore some more? Would it feel like that every time? Surely not, but then Bill seemed to think so. He had always seemed so jolly and easy going before, the life and soul of the club. I had never seen him be so serious and harsh, but then I hadn't really seen him scene more than a couple of times.

What could it hurt to go back? Well obviously, it could hurt I think as I move in bed and feel the tenderness of my arse. It was a good hurt though, I wriggle again just to feel the sensation, I'm instantly back in the club feeling the cane that put the bruising there. I want to experience that feeling again. There was no way I could just leave it at this one night, I would go back on Friday and see what happened.

I want to know exactly what sort of a relationship Bill was suggesting, was he just wanting an occasional scene or something more? There was only one way to find out. Club Entice was calling to me and I would have to respond.

# BILL

Friday night again, would she be back? She had been wandering through my mind all week. The queue of people waiting to sign in is a long one, it's looking like tonight is going to be busy. I look up from the desk to see Adam and Elissa next in the line.

"Good evening you two, how are you tonight?" I smile at Elissa, but she still looks nervously at me.

"Evening Bill, it looks like a busy one tonight." Adam shakes my hand.

"Yes, lots of people in already. Leo and Gemma are already inside." Elissa's face lights up when I tell them that.

"Will Holly be joining you tonight?" Adam asks

"She better be or I will be going to find her." I laugh.

Elissa gasps at my words and I turn to look closely at her. I need to sort this out now, she has been looking at me differently since she watched me scene with Holly and she shouldn't, I'm still the same person.

"Now Elissa, stop looking at me as though I'm an axe murderer. I'm still the same Bill you met the first night you came in here."

A red flush sweeps over her face, and she looks to Adam.

"You may speak freely little mouse." He looks amused by the whole thing.

"I'm sorry, you just looked so mean and scary last week, I thought I'd read you wrong, or missed something." She looks sheepish.

"Did Adam not explain about Sadists?" I ask.

"He did yes, but I still don't understand it. How can someone enjoy feeling pain like that?"

"I explained all this pet, just because we don't enjoy that much pain doesn't mean others can't enjoy it." Adam explains gently.

"Look, why don't you speak to Holly about it when she arrives, she might be able to explain how she felt during the scene." I say.

"If she comes back." Adam laughs.

"She will, she's seen what she can find in here now, she won't be able to turn her back on it." I say confidently.

"Or you." Elissa smiles at me.

"That's the plan." I smile back at her.

I watch them go through the door into the club room with more than a little envy, the love they shared was beautiful to see, it was the same with Gemma and Leo. I never thought I would want the same thing again, but I am tired of being lonely.

I check in several more people before the person I am waiting for steps through the door. She looks stunning, dressed in an electric blue corset dress and high heels. She also looks nervous, but at least she had still come.

She walks up to the desk and stands with her hands behind her back and her head lowered.

"Very nice girly. It's good to see you, have you had enough time to think about our scene last week?"

"Yes Sir."

"What are your thoughts?"

"I'm still confused about what exactly you are suggesting, but I enjoyed the scene so much. I want to explore more, but I'm nervous and a bit scared of messing up again." A very honest answer, that is good.

"We will talk more a bit later, but I am glad you came back, you aren't the only one who enjoyed last week girly."

"I almost didn't come." She admitted in a whisper.

"Oh, I know. Now off you go into the play room, I will be in later when I can get someone to cover the desk. I want you to sit with Elissa and Gemma, Elissa wants to talk to you and I don't want you talking to any other Dom's. Is that clear?"

"Yes Sir." She walks past me and through the door to the club room.

I need to find someone to cover me on the desk, the need to get my canes out is already starting to build.

# HOLLY

The door closes behind me, shutting me into the club room. It's busy, but not too overcrowded. Looking around I can see quite a few familiar faces, most of them are looking at me with disapproval. I scan the room looking for Gemma and Elissa. I can't imagine what Elissa wants to talk to me about, it wouldn't surprise me if she never wanted to speak to me again.

I spot them on the other side of the bar, they are deep in conversation and their Doms are sat on the adjacent sofa chatting quietly. I make my way over to them and stop nervously a few paces away from them. I have no idea what to say, I have no words, but Bill had told me to talk to them until he came in, so I had no choice but to at least try.

I am about to give up and go to find a quiet corner to hide in when Elissa looks up and sees me standing there like an idiot.

"Holly, come and join us." She smiles in welcome.

"Yes, come and have a chat." Gemma inches further up the sofa to make room for me to sit down.

I glance over at Adam and Leo to see what they think of me joining their submissives, they both have a warm welcoming look for me.

"Stop looking like they are about to kick you out, as far as we are concerned everything is finished with, you apologised and that's the end of it, we don't hold grudges." Gemma pokes me in the ribs and I jump in surprise.

"Holly, I meant it when I said I accept your apology. I also mean it when I say I hope we can be friends. I've never had many, in fact Gemma is my first one, I hope you will be my second." Elissa says, taking hold of my hand.

"That's much more than I deserve, especially from you."

"Behave, if you want to punish yourself even more then just wear cheap scratchy lace underwear for a while, it's the sub version of a hair shirt." Gemma laughs and I can't help but laugh too.

"You may as well give in you know, resistance is futile once she sets her sights on you." Leo says, smiling at his wife.

"And you would certainly know." Adam jokes.

"You two carry on your boring work chat and leave us to our girl talk." Gemma says and sticks her tongue out at Leo.

"Just you remember where we are sweetheart, you haven't had a good caning in a while." He winks at her.

I look at her with my mouth open in shock, I can't believe she just got away with that.

"Oh, she hasn't got away with it, she's going to regret it later. I'm learning that they never forget, even if you think they have." Elissa says.

"He's a pussy cat really." Gemma winks at me.

"I heard that." Leo calls from the other sofa.

"So, Bill said you wanted to talk to me?" I ask Elissa.

"I do, although I don't know where to start, or how to ask without offending you." She looks worried.

"Just ask, I promise I won't get upset."

"Well, it was about your scene with Bill last week. I thought I knew who he was, but I have to say he was so scary last week I'm beginning to think I read him wrong."

"He's not scary, he laughs and jokes a lot." I feel I need to defend him, he gave me so much last week.

"But he was so harsh with you, and your scene looked really brutal." She looks confused.

"I think what Elissa is wondering about, is what you get out of a scene like that, do you actually like it?" Gemma adds.

"Oh, I did enjoy it so much, it was everything I have been looking for. The sting of the pain sweeps everything else away, it leaves calm and clean emptiness behind."

"Have you been in a bdsm relationship before?" Elissa asks.

"No, I wasn't even sure it existed outside of the books I've read. The couple of times I've scened in here before weren't like that. Bill gave me a gift, he showed me it is out there."

"Oh, look at that, she has that glow." Gemma smiles

"What glow?" I ask

"The one that says you are hooked on the feeling you get from finding the right person for you." Elissa says dreamily.

Gemma sighs "Yep." She agrees and they both look over at their men.

"It's not like that, I don't even know what he wants." I protest.

"Tell it to someone who will believe you missy." Gemma laughs.

"No, really we haven't even talked about anything except scening again." That's what I'm really wondering, exactly what type of relationship he is proposing.

"So, you like the pain then? You get something from it? I couldn't cope with that much, let alone enjoy it."

"Elissa, it isn't a competition remember, we are all different. Some like thudy pain, some like stingy pain, some like lots of pain, some don't like any. If we were all the same it would be boring, we all just need to find someone who enjoys the same things we do." Gemma says.

"You're right, I never thought about it that way. So, you really liked it last week?" Elissa asks me.

"No, I didn't like it, I absolutely loved it, every bit of it."

"I'm glad to hear that girly, because you are about to get more of the same." Bills voice comes from behind me and I jump in surprise.

# BILL

Her reaction makes me laugh, at least she hadn't been saying anything bad about me, it sounds like she had enjoyed our scene last week. I really want to find out how deep her masochism goes. We need to talk first though, we need to establish ground rules and what we are both looking for.

She looks up at me with nervous anticipation in her eyes, I can feel Gemma and Elissa watching our interaction closely. I hope Holly has managed to put Elissa's fears to rest, if not Gemma could help explain more, although Gemma wasn't a masochist so she wouldn't be able to explain it as well as Holly.

"Come with me girly." I beckon Holly to follow me and we walk over to a quiet corner of the room. It's partially blocked off by a selection of leafy plants and it will give us some privacy.

I indicate that she should sit on the sofa and she perches right on the edge nervously.

"There's no need to be nervous just yet girly, we are only going to talk." I laugh.

"That's what makes me nervous, what are we going to talk about?" She whispers.

"Us, we are going to talk about us."

"Is there an us?" She looks up at me with huge eyes.

"I think there could be, at least in a D/s way for the moment, who knows what way this will develop, but lets just start with that shall we?"

"So, you want me to be your sub?"

"My sub and my masochist." Her pupils dilate with excitement when I say masochist.

"Are you sure?"

"I'm positive, the connection we had last week was strong, we enjoy the same type of play and we are attracted to each other."

"I never said I was attracted to you." She blurts out, then blushes a deep red.

"Don't even try that one girly, your body told me you were attracted to me, did you not make my hand all wet last week? Or was that another masochist?" No way was she going to deny this connection between us.

"I'm sorry Sir, yes I am attracted to you, but you could have any sub here falling at your feet, why me?"

"Because I admire your bravery, because I enjoy your reaction to the pain I enjoy giving, because you are a sexy woman, and most of all, because I want to."

"Oh, okay." A small smile tilts the corner of her mouth.

"There are rules though Holly and I expect them to be obeyed."

"What are the rules?"

"You will not play with anyone else while we are together, neither will I."

"That's good, I am okay with that."

"I don't like cheats and liars, so don't even bother trying."

"I don't lie, I've never lied, never will." She sounds sincere.

"You will tell me if anything gets too much, and you will talk to me about your thoughts and feelings. The S/m dynamic takes a lot of trust and communication, it's too dangerous otherwise." I won't compromise on safety.

"I will definitely tell you if it's too much, but my feelings have always been hard to share."

"Then we will need to work on that won't we."

She looks more nervous about that than any amount of pain I might deliver. Lot's of people lock their feelings away, pain could be the key to let them out.

"If you say so Sir"

"I do indeed, now I want you to go and collect my toy bag from under the desk in reception and bring it to the spanking bench on the far wall."

She jumps up and immediately rushes off in the direction of the door to reception.

I make my way back to the two couples sat watching, none of them look bothered at being caught nosing.

"Did any of you manage to lip read or do you want the low down on our conversation from me." I try to be annoyed, but I know they were just looking out for both me and Holly.

"I think we got the general gist of the conversation, but feel free to fill in the details." Adam jokes and Elissa punches him in the arm.

"Adam, behave." She sounds shocked.

"Well now little mouse, that may not have been your best move tonight. Punching your Dom will only get you one thing." He definitely has his Dom face on now.

"Yep, a very sore bum." Gemma laughs.

"I wouldn't laugh too hard sweetheart, don't forget you are due a sore bum too after what you did to my car this morning." Gemma's laughter dies in a strangled choking noise.

"What exactly did she do to your car?" I ask.

"Go on, tell them what you did." Leo orders.

"Well I may have had a slight mishap with an open pot of glitter, and some of it may have found it's way into the air vent." She try's her best to look innocent.

"It's been quite a hot day today hasn't it?" Adam says, trying not to laugh.

"It has indeed, so obviously I put the blowers on." Leo rolled his eyes.

"Oh dear Gemma, that's bad even for you." I shake my head at her.

"Well he would get bored if I didn't push him a little." She laughs.

"I don't think an hour and three shampoos to get rid of all the glitter attached to me like glue counts as a little push sweetheart. Not to mention the length of time it's going to take to de-glitter the car." He might say he's annoyed, but amusement fills his voice.

"Your life will never be dull Leo, that's for sure." I slap him on the back as I walk off to wait for Holly near the spanking bench.

## HOLLY

I open the door to reception and groan when I see Jason is manning the desk. After his reaction to me last week I wasn't looking forward to speaking with him again. I walk behind the desk trying not to catch his eye.

"Holly, could I have a quick word." His voice halts my progress.

"Yes, what about." I just want to get this over with.

"I would like to apologise, I was out of order last week, you were brave enough to come back in here to say sorry, I can be big enough to admit I was wrong and say sorry too." He does look a bit embarrassed.

"Thank you, Jason, apology accepted." I hold out my hand and he shakes it.

"Truce?"

"Of course. I must get back in there to Bill though or I'll be in trouble. Is this his toy bag?" I ask pointing to a huge black holdall against the wall.

"Yes, can you manage, it's heavy."

"I'll be fine, don't worry." I heave the bag up off the floor, it was really heavy and I struggle to carry it to the door.

I push the door open with my bum and turn into the room, letting the door click shut behind me. I look around to see exactly where the spanking bench is and seeing it I head in that direction. Just as I'm squeezing between a group of people and the wall a man steps in front of me, blocking my way.

"Excuse me, please." I say looking up to see who it is.

My heart sinks as I see it's Andrew. He was one of the men I had scened with, I hadn't enjoyed it at all and he actually made me really uncomfortable. There was just something off about him and I move to get past him.

"Hello Holly, it's nice to see you back, I hadn't realised your ban was finished." He leans closer to me and I try to lean as far away from him as I can.

"Yes, I've been back for two weeks now."

"We should play again." He says and I can smell alcohol on his breath.

"I'm sorry, but no. I can't play with anyone, I am with Bill." Again, I try to move past him.

"I'm sure he won't mind sharing." He leers

"He won't share, and I'm sorry, but I wouldn't want to scene with you again anyway, we didn't click at all really." I try and close the conversation.

"What does it matter if we click or not? You like being hit and I enjoyed hitting you."

"That's not how I work, sorry."

"Oh, I get it, you've set your sights on the boss, he doesn't own this place you know, he's only a manager."

"It wouldn't matter if he did or not, that's not why I am with him and it's certainly not why I am turning you down." I'm getting angry now. "Now please move to one side and let me pass."

He suddenly grabs my arm tight and I gasp in surprise.

"Are you okay Holly? Do you need help with the bag?" I look around to see Gemma and Elissa standing behind me.

"Oh, yes please it's really heavy. I must go now Andrew." I glare at him and he has no choice but to let go of my arm and walk away.

"What was all that about? It looked like he was hassling you." Gemma looks concerned.

"It's nothing really, I scened with him once and he was asking if I wanted to scene again." I look at my arm and see it's all red where his hand had been.

"That doesn't look like nothing, you should tell Bill." Elissa says.

"No! I don't want to be the cause of any more drama in here, I don't want to make a fuss. It's fine now, I said no and he knows I mean it, he won't ask again."

"If you're sure, but I still think Bill would want to know. He shouldn't be touching anyone who doesn't want him to." Gemma sounds angry.

"It's fine, he won't do it again. Now I really need to get this bag to Bill or I definitely will be in trouble." I rush off before they can say anything else.

I hurry as fast as I can with the heavy bag over to the bench where Bill is waiting impatiently.

"What took you so long girly?"

"I'm so sorry Sir." The words rush out.

"Did something happen? You look flustered, did someone upset you?" He lifts my chin and studies me closely.

"No, I'm sorry, Jason wanted to talk to me and then your bag was really heavy." I really don't want to tell him about Andrew.

"What did Jason say? Is he the reason you look upset?" His jaw clenches in anger.

"No, he was actually really nice. He wanted to apologise for the way he was last week. He said if I had been big enough to apologise then he needed to as well."

"Oh, okay well I'm glad he sees the error of his ways. Everyone deserves a second chance."

"He was really very respectful and I accepted his apology."

"Good girl. Now put my bag down over near the bench and strip." His face has changed into the hard Sadist face from last week and a shiver of excitement runs through me.

# BILL

Something had definitely got her flustered, was it just the embarrassment of Jason's apology? Or was there something she wasn't telling me? I decide to let it go for now, but she better not be lying to me.

I watch as she strips out of her clothes and folds them neatly on the chair at the side of the scene area. She really is beautiful, her skin looks so soft, it will look even more beautiful when it is coloured with my cane stripes. She turns to face me with her hands behind her back, head lowered, waiting for my instructions.

"Kneel on the bench girly." I wait as she gets into position on the bench.

I arrange her exactly how I want her, knees apart, breasts dangling down each side of the bench, her head resting on the cool leather, her face turned towards the room. I rest my hand between her shoulder blades until I feel the deep breath she releases and the tension leave her body.

Whatever had upset her had gone now, she was relaxed and waiting for me to take her on a journey.

I lean down so my lips are next to her ear.

"Brace yourself girly, I'm going to take you somewhere you haven't even dreamed existed." I whisper, and I feel a tremor run through her.

I trail my hand down the curve of her spine, to rest on the smooth cheek of her arse. I want to prolong the anticipation of pain, I want to wait until just the right moment to deliver the first blow. I watch her closely, she is so still, waiting for me. How long will I have to wait for her?

I wait and watch with my hand still on her arse. After about a minute I see the flicker I have been waiting for. Just the slightest movement that say's she is about turn her head to see what I am doing. I bring my hand down hard on her arse and watch with satisfaction as redness blooms outwards and she flinches.

Bringing my hand down over and over with increasing hardness, until she is squirming on the bench in front of me, I lean down to whisper in her ear again.

"You will be still girly."

Instantly she stills and I feel a rush of pleasure at her instinctive submission.

I choose a hard-wooden paddle from my toy bag and stroke her pink skin with it. A shiver runs through her and goose bumps erupt across her body. I use the paddle hard on both cheeks and I hear her sigh in relaxed contentment. I feel so in tune with her, I feel every breath she takes.

The smack of the paddle rings out between us in a song of giving and acceptance. She accepts each blow as the gift I intend it to be and it's beautiful. I crouch down next to her head and look deep into her eyes. She has the drifting happy look of a sub well on the way to subspace, time to push her limits a little.

"Are you ready girly?" I ask with a smile.

Her lips curve in an answering smile.

"Yes please Sir." She sighs.

"Okay then, here we go." I stand and pull two canes from my bag.

The cane whooshes through the air and she tenses when she hears it coming. That's the worst thing she could have done. The sting will rebound through muscles held taught doubling the pain. A shocked gasp escapes her control and I smile, now we're getting somewhere.

The thin cane delivers sting after sting, leaving a red stripe wherever it lands. Her body relaxes as she absorbs the sting of each blow. The more pain I deliver, the more she relaxes into it. The room has disappeared now, it's just me and her, connected together in our own space in the world. I see when she gasps, when she sighs in contentment, when she needs more, when I should let her breathe for a few seconds. The flow of the scene is magical.

I change to the thicker cane, this will give a deeper thudding sensation and she should be able to relax into it more. I run my hand over her skin, checking to make sure it isn't close to splitting. I definitely don't want to draw blood or leave any permanent marks.

At the first blow from the thicker cane, her back arches with pleasure and a low groan sounds deep in her throat. Oh yes, she loves the deeper pain. I rein even, firm strokes across her arse in a steady rhythm.

# HOLLY

My head is filled with pain, it has pushed everything else out until only the pain is left. It's so beautiful in its absolute simplicity, it fills all the empty spaces inside me, warming me from inside, just as it heats the skin of my arse.

Each time the cane lands, it pushes me further away into the beautiful floating sensation. I feel no panic to cling to reality, I want to see how far I can go in my little bubble of sensation. This is what I had been searching for, and Bill has given it to me. I feel his hand on my cheek and I slowly open my eyes to look at him.

"How are you coping girly? Still okay?" He asks.

"hmmmm"

"Almost there then." He smiles.

His hand pushes my head back down onto the bench and begins again with the cane. I feel as though I am on the edge of something monumental, something just out of reach that I can't see. I strain towards whatever it is, trying to capture it, but it seems to keep bobbing away, just out of reach.

"Stop reaching girly, just let it come to you." His voice washes over me and I melt into the bench, giving up the struggle.

The next blow of the cane lands and I follow the flow of sensation further into my bubble.

"That's the way girly, follow the pain, it will take you to the right place." His cane is leading me, his voice is pushing me, towards the elusive place in my head.

The next stroke of his cane explodes in my head and my world shatters into millions of glittering shiny pieces. I am lost in a bubble of glittering sensation where only pure beauty exists. I can't seem to find my body anymore, I don't know where I am.

I become aware of a new sensation, a gentle stroking warmth, and I slowly become aware that I have skin. Someone is stroking gently down my back and across my tender bottom. I shiver and suddenly a soft warmth surrounds me. I give up the struggle to figure it out and just relax into the softness with a sigh.

I have no idea how much time has passed before I become aware of arms holding me tight, a strong chest under my head, and a rumbling laugh vibrating against my ear.

Slowly I become aware of other things, the rumble of voices around me and the slap of leather against skin. I wriggle and pain shoots across my arse, I yelp and a loud laugh comes from the hard chest beneath me.

I open my eyes and look out over the blanket I'm wrapped in, I am cradled in Bill's arms as he talks quietly with Adam and Leo. I am comforted by his understated care, he isn't making a fuss, but he is watching me, caring for me, keeping me safe.

I would be happy to stay here like this forever.

The world is creeping back in though, I can hear the sounds of people playing in the room and the jarring sound of people talking and laughing at the bar. I want to go back to the happy peaceful place I was before.

I look up at Bill and he's studying me closely.

"How are you feeling girly?"

"I'm okay." I cringe at a loud shout from the bar area.

"I would like an honest answer girly, not the answer you think I want."

Oh my, he's not going to let me get away with anything.

"I feel shaky."

A group of people walk past us all laughing loudly and I cringe further into the blanket and the shelter of his arms.

"The noise is bothering you." It's a statement not a question.

"I'm sorry Sir." I feel pathetic.

"You have nothing to be sorry for Holly. That was a really intense scene, aftercare should be whatever you need it to be, and you obviously need quiet." He brushes my cheek softly with his warm hand.

Suddenly he stands up lifting me into his arms.

"Where are we going Sir?"

"Somewhere quiet."

"But, don't you need to watch the desk?" I'm taking too much of his time.

"I have someone watching the desk and I need to watch you."

## BILL

I have a sudden need to be alone with the luscious Holly. I nod at Adam and Leo as I pass and carry Holly over to the door marked private behind the bar. She rests her head against my chest, total trust, such a precious gift.

I walk down the corridor to my flat and turn the lamp on filling the lounge with a warm glow. Her eyes are huge and ever so slightly out of focus, as I lay her against the cushions on the sofa. She snuggles further into the blanket with a shiver, so I light the fire to warm the room.

I sit down, pulling her into my arms to rest against my chest.

"Is this better?" I ask softly.

"Yes, thank you Sir."

"You were amazing girly." I am astounded by the trust she has gifted me.

"I didn't do anything." She mumbles

"You put your trust in me, you allowed me to take you somewhere special. That's everything." I kiss her head softly.

"But you gave me so much." She frowns up at me.

"I wouldn't frown at your Dom like that girly." I snap, moving to pin her hands over her head on the arm of the sofa.

Her gasp shows more than surprise, and her dilated pupils speak of excitement and desire. I look down at her, taking in how beautiful she looks, all aroused and gasping. My cock hardens, and I lean down to kiss her. Her groan fills my mouth and I deepen the kiss.

Her arms twine around my neck and she tries to pull me closer.

"Don't forget who's in charge here girly." I growl at her.

Her eyes drift open and she struggles to focus on my face.

"Sorry Sir." She whispers, lowering her eyes.

"That's better, now put your arms over the arm of the sofa and leave them there."

"Yes Sir." Her eyes are huge as she moves her arms into position.

"Good girl." Her cheeks warm at the compliment.

She really is a true submissive and she is blossoming under my attention and praise.

I flick open the blanket, revealing her lush breasts to my gaze. Her peach coloured nipples tighten and thrust towards me, begging me to taste them. I lower my head till my lips are almost touching the peaked flesh, then I blow on the sensitive peak.

Her back arches towards me pushing her nipple closer to my mouth, and she whimpers with need.

"Don't move girly, or you won't get what you need." I threaten.

"Please Sir, I need." She whines.

"What do you need?" I ask.

"I need you."

"I'm here."

"I need more, need you to fuck me." She pants.

I close my lips over her turgid nipple and suck it hard into my mouth. Her groan is one of pure satisfaction.

"You like that?"

"Oh god yes."

I suck her nipple back into my mouth and press it hard against the roof of my mouth, her answering groan sends shivers down my spine. I reach into the chest at the side of the sofa and pull out a pair of clamps.

"I think you might like these even more." I hold up the clamps for her to see.

A worried look crosses her face.

"Nipple clamps?" She asks.

"That's right girly."

Clipping the clamp to her distended nipple I watch her face for signs of it being too much for her. She gasps at the bite of pain, but her pupils dilate with desire, she likes the pain so much.

I attach the second clamp to her other nipple, then brush my palm over both at the same time, she whimpers when my hand disturbs the clamps, causing them to bite more on her abused flesh. Reaching into the box again I pull out a third clamp and hold it up for her to see.

"What's that one for." Her eyes widen.

"I'm sure you can guess Holly." I laugh softly.

"Oh….." realisation dawns and she unconsciously closes her legs.

"Oh, I don't think so girly, open your legs for me." I command.

"But, please Sir." She begs.

"Now Holly, or I will restrain them open." I threaten.

Hesitantly, she slowly opens her legs slightly.

"Further." I demand.

She huffs in irritation, but then moves her legs further apart, leaning down I run my tongue over her clit and she groans, I suckle on her pink swollen nub until it peaks out from its protective hood.

"Now that's a pretty sight." I blow gently over her pussy and she shivers in anticipation.

I attach the clamp and tighten it over the delicate nub, loosening it slightly when I see her eyes tighten in pain. I lick her clit again and she hisses as the sensation hits.

## HOLLY

My body is on fire, my nipples feel tight and pinched and my pussy throbs with the beat of my heart. I had thought my pleasure and sensation for the night was over, it seems he has other ideas.

"I know you love the pain girly, but now I need to know if you want to take this further." What did he mean?

"More pain you mean?" I ask confused.

"Yes, but I also need to know if you want to take this further sexually, and emotionally." Oh God yes, I did.

"Yes, I do."

"I'm talking about a real relationship Holly, not just a play arrangement." He sounds so serious.

"You mean, like dating? Boyfriend and Girlfriend?" I need to know exactly what he means now, it doesn't sound like he's just talking about sex.

"I think what we could have is more intense than that, but yes. You would be mine and I would be your Sir, your Master, your Sadist, your lover." He punctuates each title with a kiss across my body.

He was talking about the type of relationship Elissa had with Adam and Gemma had with Leo, he was talking about the type of relationship I have been yearning for. He was everything I had been hoping to find, he made me feel good, he understood my need for pain, and he was offering me everything I wanted. Could I possibly be this lucky?

"I want to take this further, I want to see where this could go."

He smiles at me, then looks down the length of my body and his smile turns into an evil grin.

"Okay girly, lets play. You are not allowed to come until I give you permission, your orgasms belong to me now."

All my breath leaves me in a whoosh, and I feel myself become wetter. This suddenly sounded a lot more serious.

Taking a deep breath, I look up into his face and he smiles slowly down at me, looking over my body as though he is trying to decide where to play first. His hand slaps against my clamped clit with a loud crack and I arch my back at the stinging sensation.

"Oh, you do like the pain don't you girly?" He laughs.

He slaps his hand against my swollen flesh again and again, until I'm groaning and my thighs are wet with desire.

"Don't come Holly, not until I tell you to."

"Please, please Sir." I whine.

"We've only just got started girly, there's a long way to go before you'll get your orgasm." He laughs.

I might never survive, I already feel desperate. It must be because of our scene earlier, all the sensations adding together to bring me to the edge so quickly. He runs the tip of his finger along the crease of my thigh and I shiver in anticipation.

My eyes drift closed as I feel his hot breath fan over my pussy, tickling and making me squirm. His tongue runs over my clit, disturbing the clamp and making me gasp as stinging sensation shoots over my skin. His finger pushes inside me as his lips close over my clit and I groan at the dual sensation.

He adds a second finger, stretching me and pushing me closer to orgasm. His teeth graze over my clit and I feel it swell as more blood rushes to it.

"Please Sir, let me come." I beg.

"Not yet Holly, be patient." His words rumble through my pussy filling me with need.

His finger thrusts in and out of my soaking pussy, until I'm right on the edge of orgasm, the moment stretches out for an eternity with me poised on the very edge of satisfaction. Then he pulls his fingers out and slaps my pussy hard. Scorching heat flares over my body and I arch upwards from the sofa towards his mouth.

His hands press me back down and hold me still, and I groan in disappointment as the orgasm escapes my grasp. I was so close and now it's gone.

"Please, I need it, please Sir." I look up at him with pleading eye's.

"Soon Holly, you'll enjoy it more if you wait a little longer."

"But, Sir please."

He just looks down at me with a smile on his face and thrusts his fingers back into my pussy. My arousal peaks again and I'm instantly on the edge of coming again. Again, he holds me on the edge for endless minutes, licking at my clit with his firm tongue and thrusting his fingers ruthlessly in and out of my sopping pussy.

Sweat dampens my skin and my hair sticks to my face as I strain for the orgasm just out of reach.

# BILL

She is stunning in her surrender and submission. Laid out before me for my pleasure, waiting for me to give her the release she is craving, at my mercy and under my control. My cock throbs with the need to be inside her, but I hold myself back, pushing her deeper into the need I can see burning through her.

This is a need I haven't felt before, this need to possess someone so totally, heart and body and soul. She has come to mean so much to me in such a short time, it's scary. As the thought passes through my mind the fear settles deep into the pit of my stomach, what if she doesn't feel the same? What if this is just playing to her? Just scratching an itch?

Pushing the unwelcome thoughts away I focus on the writhing woman beneath me, she's poised right on the edge of orgasm, waiting for me to push her over the edge, waiting for whatever I decide to gift to her.

My fingers brush lightly over her clit and she groans deep in her throat, trying to lift her hips closer to my touch, but then remembering the rules and trying to resist moving.

"Such a good girl!" I murmur against her swollen flesh.

I reach into the box again and pull out a glass dildo, it's cold and hard and it will feel even colder against her burning pussy. She gasps in shock when I push it deep into her pussy in one hard long thrust.

"It's cold." She protests

"It is isn't it?" I laugh.

She mutters something under her breath, it doesn't sound like a compliment.

"What was that girly?" I grip her jaw hard so she has no choice but to look me in the eye.

Her eyes slowly focus on me, then widen as she realises she said whatever it was out loud.

"I called you a sadist." She says with a little bit of defiance to her tone.

Laughter bursts from me, startling her.

"Well I thought you knew that already." I felt good to laugh with someone like this.

"I might have forgotten for a second." She smiles up at me, her face flushed, her eyes sparkling with desire, and suddenly I want to give her the world.

"Then perhaps I should remind you girly." I harden my expression and her eyes widen with anticipation and desire.

I slap the palm of my hand against one breast, then the other, two sharp stings of pain to focus us both again. Then I slap her clit hard, her gasp is still one of pleasure, definitely a true masochist.

I pull a riding crop off the shelf under the coffee table and gently stroke her jaw with the leather tab at its end. Her eyes are fixed on mine now, I have her total attention, her chest rises and falls rapidly as her breath comes in quick excited pants. I stretch the moment to it's limit, waiting until I sense she is about to break the tension and move.

There it is, the slight tightening of her eyes, the sudden tension in the muscles of her stomach.

I pull the dildo out until just the tip is at her entrance, then I slap her clit with the riding crop and plunge the dildo back in to the hilt. Her scream fills the room and she arches against the arm of the sofa, her head back, the cords of her neck standing out as she strains towards the sensations filling her.

I wish I could capture the image for eternity, the total beauty of her surrender to the feelings rushing through her, that I have given her, it's breath taking.

Pulling the dildo out again, I slap the crop down hard just above the clamp on her clit, and again plunge the dildo back in. I find the rhythm, pull out, slap, plunge in, over and over again until she is sobbing and begging for her release.

"Please.......Sir please, I can't, it's too much."

"You can Holly, look at me girly." I slide over her body and she gasps as the denim of my trousers abrades her tender swollen pussy.

It takes a while for her eyes to focus on me, she is lost in a world of sensation, but eventually I see she is back with me.

"There you are! Such a good girl, do you want your reward now Holly?" I gently kiss her parted lips, bringing her slowly back down from the dizzying heights of pain.

"Sir, I feel floaty." She whispers.

"I know girly, it's a good place to be isn't it?"

"Feels good." She slurs

"Are you ready for me now?"

"I need you." She groans.

I pull away from her and she whimpers in protest.

"Don't worry, you're going to get all of me, I just need to get rid of these clothes." I chuckle

It only takes a few seconds to strip and grab a condom from the table and I'm back covering her body with the heat of mine. Pulling the dildo from her pussy I let my finger slide over folds slick with desire. She groans again and I know I can't stretch this out much longer, one of us might explode if I tried.

I rip the condom packet with my teeth and cover my cock, hissing as the touch sends me closer to the edge. I rub my cock over her labia, coating myself with her essence, making her groan deep in her throat.

"Look at me now Holly, keep your eyes on me." She obeys instantly.

I slowly push my cock in until her heat envelopes me from base to tip, our gazes locked in an intense stare, as I bottom out, deep in her pussy, a sigh leaves us both. A sigh of total satisfaction, of rightness, of being home.

A single tear leaks from her eye to roll down her cheek as she looks at me.

"Holly are you hurt? Is it too much?" I ask concerned I'd pushed her too far.

"No Sir, it's beautiful." She smiles up at me.

"Well while you are still thinking that, lets remove these shall we?" I say as I unclip the first nipple clamp.

Her breath hisses out and a deep flush spreads across her face.

"Fuck!"

"That hurts doesn't it girly?" I laugh and remove the other clamp.

"Ouch, fuck that hurts so much." She is panting now and I lower my head to suck each nipple in turn, extending the sensation for as long as possible.

"I bet you can't wait to see what it feels like when I take the clamp off your clit can you?" Her eyes widen, but I can feel her pussy clench around me at the thought.

I start to move, pulling slowly out, then just as slowly pushing back in, until she is gasping her eyes are glazed again. When I can see she is getting close to the edge again I speed up my movements, thrusting in and out, harder each time until I'm hammering in and out of her swollen pussy.

I can feel her juices running down over my balls to drip on the floor at my feet and I growl with satisfaction. Her eyes are squeezed tightly shut and she's tossing her head from side to side.

"Look at me Holly." I order and her heavy eye lids slowly lift, showing me eyes filled with passion and wildness.

I hold still, eyes locked on hers as I reach down and unclip the clamp from her clit. Her scream fills the room, sending shivers down my spine and up through my balls to my cock. I can feel myself get even harder, even bigger as I plunge in and out like a wild man.

I can feel her coming over and over again, gripping my cock so tight it's hard to pull out. My hands grip her shoulders, stopping her moving with the force of my thrusts, and the next time I plunge in I pull her down towards me. She screams my name and I feel her squirt her release, covering my stomach and balls with hot cum. I let go and plunge in and out of her hot body, feeling the tingle of orgasm spread over me, my balls tighten and it feels like the top of my head is about to explode. Wave after wave of cum pulses from my cock, filling the condom as I shout my release.

# HOLLY

The room is dark and quiet when I wake up, I'm not sure where I am for a minute. Where ever it is, it's very comfy and warm. I stretch and feel a warm hard body against my back, Bill. The details of last night come rushing back and I sigh in contentment. Have I ever felt this good before? Not that I can remember.

I don't remember moving from the sofa to a bed, Bill must have carried me and cleaned me up a bit too from the feel of things. He had pushed me so far last night, but I had felt so safe with him. He said he wants a real relationship, with me, I'd never expected this outcome when I'd come back here to apologise.

I can feel his warm breath on the back of my neck, it's comforting. I relax even more into his arms and let my eyes drift closed again. A bit more sleep would be nice after such a big night.

Next time I wake I'm alone in the bed and sunlight is streaming in through the window. I stretch out and take a quick inventory of my body and all it's sore bits. Not too bad considering, my arse is a little tender and my nipples are sore when they brush against the sheet, but other than that there is only the small ache of seldom used muscles between my legs.

I can hear Bill moving around in the kitchen, and a few minutes later the smell of coffee drifts into the bedroom. Wrapping the sheet around me I head into the bathroom, a quick shower later I head out to the kitchen still wrapped in the sheet. I have no idea where my clothes are, they could even still be in the club room. How embarrassing was it going to be coming home mid-morning in my corset and short skirt?

Standing in the kitchen doorway I watch Bill as he moves around, putting breakfast items on the small round table. He looks so different from the Dominant Sadist of the night before, he could be any man preparing breakfast on a Saturday morning. I'd never made the connection between club life and every day life before, it was surprising to see that people can do both.

"Morning." I say hesitantly.

Bill looks up from putting the butter on the table with a huge grin.

"Good morning Holly, did you sleep well?" Such a mundane question after the intensity of the night before.

"Yes, thank you, what time is it?"

"It's just after ten, you slept in." He smiles.

"It must have been late when I fell asleep though." I feel my face flush.

"Hey, there's nothing wrong with sleeping in on a Saturday, especially after such a big night." He pulls a chair out and gestures for me to sit.

"Can I help with anything?" I feel awkward just sitting here.

"No, everything is just about ready. Plus, I don't think my nerves could stand you moving around too much dressed in my bed sheet." He winks at me and turns to grab the coffee pot.

I try and tuck the sheet more firmly around me as I take the cup of coffee and add milk and sugar. As I reach for a slice of toast however I can feel the sheet begin to slip, but with my hands full I can't stop gravity from taking effect. I try to put the cup down before my assets are revealed in the glare of the sunny morning, but the cup hits the edge of the table and hot coffee sloshes over my bare feet under the table.

"Shit!" I jump up and the sheet falls all the way off as I jump about in pain.

"Holly, are you okay." His face is full of concern.

Oh god it burns, my jumping around isn't doing anything to calm the heat and tears begin to fall.

"It hurts, it's burning." I can feel myself beginning to panic and I can't seem to remember what I need to do.

"Holly!" He shouts at me, grabbing my shoulders. "Be still."

Suddenly the panic recedes and I am just left with the pain and a feeling of embarrassment.

"Bathroom, now." He spins me around and pushes me towards the bathroom.

I realise he's just got a front row seat view of my arse as he follows me into the small room.

"Sit, now." He points to the edge of the bath and turns the shower head to cold. "Swing your feet into the bath girly."

He angles the shower head to point at my foot and the cold water sooths the burning instantly.

"Thank you, that feels better. I'm sorry I panicked."

"You need to leave the water running over it for at least fifteen minutes so it doesn't blister."

"Yes Sir." I say automatically.

"It's Bill outside of the club room or the bedroom Holly."

"But, I thought…"

"Holly, I am Dominant and I am a Sadist, but I don't want a slave twenty-four seven, that's exhausting. I want a partner, someone who will have the guts to argue with me if I'm being an idiot."

"Really?" I say with a giggle.

"Really! Trust me it does happen sometimes."

"It's confusing, I'm only used to you in the club, in Dom mode." He seems so normal.

"You'll get used to it. How does your foot feel now?"

"Cold."

"It doesn't look like it will blister, I think we caught it in time." He turns the water off and reaches for a towel from the rail.

I hold my hand out to take the towel from him, but he shakes his head and holds it out of reach.

"Give me your foot Holly." He holds his hand out and I lift my foot to rest in his palm.

It's only then I remember I am still naked and he will now be able to see all my personal bits. I look away, blushing.

"Really? You're going to be all embarrassed after everything we did last night?" He laughs.

BILL

She really is still shy; her blush is cute. I gently pat her foot dry with the towel and check it again for any blistering. It doesn't look too bad now, just a bit of redness across the top of her foot.

"Where are my clothes?" She asks looking around as though they will suddenly appear.

"They're in a bag in the hallway, but I can probably find you something to wear more suitable for a Saturday morning."

"Thank you, I was thinking it would be embarrassing arriving home dressed like that in daylight."

"Go pour yourself some fresh coffee and I'll go see what I can find." I think there are still some of Hannah's things in the back of the wardrobe.

As I walk back into the kitchen I can hear her talking to someone on the phone.

"Are you sure? Me?" she asks whoever is on the other end.

"Well, okay, what time?"

She pulls the sheet around her shoulders as she listens to the reply.

"All right, I'll see you there then. Are you really sure though?"

I put the clothes over the back of the chair and pour myself a fresh cup of coffee, then I sit and wait for her to finish the call.

"Okay, well I'll see you later then. Bye." She hangs up looking at her phone in confusion.

"Problem?" I ask.

"No, I'm just confused." She looks up at me, I just wait, if she wants to tell me she will.

"That was Gemma, she was calling to ask me to go shopping with her and Elissa this afternoon."

"And this confuses you why?" I ask.

"Well, for two reasons really. Why would they want to invite me, and how did they get hold of my number?" She sips her coffee

"I'm not sure how they got your number, except to say Gemma is a very determined woman when she's after something. As to why they would ask you to go with them, well why not?"

"Well I don't really know them and after what I did I wouldn't expect them to want to spend any more time with me than they had to." She says as though I'm being especially silly.

"Holly, Gemma and Elissa aren't like that, they are lovely women and neither of them make friends with just anyone. If they've invited you to go shopping it's simply because they want to be your friend."

"Do you think so?" She looks so vulnerable, sat there with the bed sheet wrapped around her.

"I know so, just go and enjoy yourself. Not that you'll have much choice if I know Gemma. She makes shopping look like an Olympic sport." I laugh.

"Okay then, I'll go."

"Good girl. Will you have dinner with me tonight?" I ask.

"Don't you need to work tonight?"

"Only from about nine, if we have an early dinner you could keep me company on the front desk." I would enjoy having her next to me while I work.

"Dinner would be lovely, thank you, but I don't want to get in your way while you're working."

"I would like you there, unless you have something else you need to be doing."

"No, I would only be watching TV otherwise."

"That's settled then, I'll pick you up at six thirty for dinner." I reach for a piece of toast and watch her face as she sips her coffee.

She still looks a bit shell shocked, but then a lot has happened since she walked into the club last night. I will have to watch her closely for any signs of sub drop. It was a distinct possibility after a heavy scene like the one we had last night.

She had been glorious in her submission and she had needed the pain and sensation just as much as I had enjoyed giving it to her. The way she had continued to submit to me when we fucked was the icing on the cake. She really was perfect.

We share a relaxed breakfast and then she goes to freshen up and get dressed. I'm glad Gemma and Elissa have decided to befriend her, she is a lovely woman who could use a few friends, I get the impression she doesn't really have any.

She comes back into the kitchen and it doesn't bother me as much as I thought it would to see her in Hannah's clothes. I walk around the table and pull her into my arms for a long slow kiss. She melts into the kiss and a low groan tells me she is as turned on as I am. I nip at her bottom lip as I pull away and she gasps at the small pinch of pain.

"I am looking forward to dinner later."

"Me too." She whispers.

"You better get going or you'll be late for Gemma and Elissa." I nudge her towards the hallway, picking up the bag with her clothes as we pass.

"I wouldn't want to keep them waiting, although I still don't know why they invited me."

"Just go with the flow of the force of nature that is Gemma." I laugh. "I'll see you at six thirty for dinner."

"Yes Sir….. I mean Bill." She looks at me confused and then grabs the bag of clothes and rushes out of the door.

## HOLLY

I look nervously at my reflection in the rear-view mirror, my makeup looks ok, at least it's not smudged. Taking a deep breath, I get out of the car and walk towards the entrance to the shopping centre. It feels like my first night back in the club all over again. I wonder if I'm walking into a revenge situation. Maybe they want to humiliate me, like Amy did to Elissa.

I look around as I get closer to the café Gemma said they would meet me at, I can't see them. Perhaps this is the joke, maybe they are watching from some hidden place, laughing at me as I wait for them. I'll give them five more minutes and then I will leave. They probably deserve five minutes of my humiliation.

"Hey Holly, sorry we're a bit late." I spin around to see them both doing a half run down the stairs from the upper level.

"It's my fault." Gemma gushes as they come to a sudden stop right in front of me.

"It's okay, I've only been here a few minutes." I reassure them.

"Gemma was a little tied up at home, she was a bit naughty the other day and Leo decided today was punishment time." Elissa laughs.

"It wasn't that naughty really." Gemma says with a cheeky grin.

"What did you do?" I ask.

"I just tied pretty ribbons to the handles of all his floggers and canes." She says with a wink.

Elissa is giggling and I can't help but smile at them, they are like two naughty children.

"Well we're here now, shall we go in?" Elissa gestures to the café and we walk to the hostess station.

"Table for three ladies?" The hostess greets us with a practiced smile.

She leads us to a table in the corner and hands us all a menu. We order some drinks and study the menu as she leaves to get them.

I can't help glancing at them both while they are deciding what to order. Part of me still thinks this is a big joke at my expense, but I can't seem to begrudge them that even if it is.

"Don't look so worried, we come in peace." I look up to see Gemma smiling at me.

"I don't even deserve your notice, let alone your time."

"Will you stop with that already? We've been through this, it's over and done with, I've moved on and so should you." Elissa says with a note of exasperation in her tone.

I look at her face for any hint of her still holding onto it all, but all I see is relaxed happiness.

"Okay then, I'll do my best."

"Okay, that's enough of the mushy stuff, we really want all the saucy details about you and Bill." Gemma chips in, breaking the mood totally.

I burst out laughing and Elissa joins in.

"Hey I mean it, come on dish the dirt."


"Aren't you even a little bit scared of him?" Elissa asks once we get our laughter under control.

"No, I'm scared in case it all goes wrong, in case I mess up again, but I'm not scared of Bill." I realise it's true as I say it.

"I thought he was a sweet funny man, until I saw you two scene for the first time, it looked so brutal and he looked so mean." Elissa whispers.

"He gave me exactly what I needed." I smile.

"I know you think you needed punishing, but you really didn't you know."

"No, it wasn't a punishment, he set me free. The pain sets me free." I don't know if I'm explaining it right, I don't even really understand it myself.

"You really enjoy all that pain? I mean, I enjoy some pain, flogging and spanking, but that was so much pain."

"Adam explained this to you Elissa." Gemma says.

"I know, but I still don't understand it."

"Okay, let me try and explain it, but I've never tried before, I'm only just beginning to understand it myself."

They both look up as the waitress delivers our drinks.

"Are you ready to order ladies?" she asks with a smile.

"Oh no, I didn't look yet." Elissa exclaims.

"I'll give you a few more minutes." The waitress says walking away again.

"Let's decide what to order, then I'll explain." I say, and we all study the menu in silence for the next few minutes.

After we have given our order they both look at me with interested looks on their faces.

"Okay, when I feel pain, it's like a shower of sensation that washes me clean. It clears everything away until the only thing left in my mind is the pure clear pain. I can relax and be at peace, my mind is empty and I can float along on the pain." I blush, maybe they will think I'm a weirdo.

"I feel that when we scene and Adam flogs me, but the amount of pain you seem to enjoy would be way too much for me." Elissa says.

"And me." Gemma agrees. "But we are all different. Some of us are hard wired that way and there's nothing we can do about it." She smiles at me gently.

"You don't think it means I'm a freak?" This is the main worry I still have.

"Nope, it makes you a masochist." Gemma says just as the waitress appears with our food.

She stammers as she puts our plates down and walks away blushing.

"Oops, my bad." Gemma clamps her hand over her mouth.

"Guess we won't be eating here again." Elissa laughs.

Laughter bubbles around the table as we all begin eating. It feels so good to be so relaxed with them both. They had every reason to hate me, but they seemed to like me. Things were really looking up, I now had a Dom, a lover and is seemed two friends.

We spent the afternoon strolling around the shops and generally having fun. By the time I got home I was exhausted, but happy. I still had time for a nap before I had to get ready for dinner with Bill. I hang my new dress on the wardrobe door, then set an alarm, before getting into bed with a sigh.

# BILL

Well this is new for me, picking a sub up for a dinner date. I can't actually remember the last time I went on a date. I spend time with women at the club, but an actual date, it had been years. I don't understand why I feel so drawn to the little masochist, it's not like I have a shortage of women to scene with.

Maybe it is just because she calls to the Sadist in me. Or maybe it was the fact that she wasn't actually asking anything from me. Most of the women I scened with were looking to see what I could do for them, Holly seemed surprised every time I offered her my time. She had been the same with Elissa and Gemma though. Maybe she didn't feel like she deserved to be liked.

I walk up to her front door and ring the bell, her house is small, but neat and tidy, she's planted colourful plants in the pots around the door, it makes the house look cheerful. I can hear her coming to the door and I realise I'm looking forward to spending the evening with her, much more than I ever thought I would.

The door opens and she takes my breath away, standing there in a red silky dress, her hair loose about her shoulders, her feet encased in a sinfully high pair of heels.

"Outfits like that should be outlawed." I look her up and down in appreciation.

"What's wrong with it? I didn't know where we are going, should I change?" she stammers, turning to go back inside.

"Stop!" I growl. "The dress is perfect. You look amazing."

Her blush is instant and she lowers her head in embarrassment.

"Thank you, Sir."

"We are going out for a vanilla evening Holly, you may call me Bill until we arrive at the club."

"Oh, okay, where are we going?" she reaches for her bag from the table and pulls a wrap from the hook behind the door.

"To a little Italian place I know not too far from the club. I eat there quite often on nights I'm working." I take her arm as she steps out of the house and locks the door.

"Don't you cook for yourself?" she asks in a teasing tone.

I grab a handful of her soft hair and yank her head back.

"Just because we are on a vanilla date girly, doesn't mean I will let you get away with being cheeky." I growl.

Her gasp sends blood rushing to my cock and I pull her head back a little further so I can kiss her parted lips. She groans as I deepen the kiss and I can feel her press closer to me, she's almost rubbing herself against my cock and it's my turn to groan.

I pull her head away, nibbling her plump bottom lip as I do.

"Come on girly, or we won't make it to dinner." I slap her behind as she precedes me down the front path.

She definitely puts an extra wiggle in her walk as she goes, sending the skirt of her dress swirling.

Sassy sub, she brings a smile to my face as I imagine the fun I'm going to have punishing all that sass. I'm glad she feels comfortable enough to let that bit of it escape.

In the car she's quiet again and I wonder what made her withdraw.

"How was your afternoon with Elissa and Gemma?" I hope they didn't upset her.

Her whole face lights up and she steals my breath again.

"We had so much fun, they are so lovely."

"They are, I thought you would have fun."

"Gemma is a demon shopper." She laughs

"I'll take your word for it, I've never seen her in action, but I've heard stories." She giggles at the look on my face. "I'm glad you had a good time, she won't let you escape now you know."

"I get that impression yes." Again, with the cute giggle.

It's only now, seeing her so relaxed, that I realise just how tense she always is. Apart from when we have scened, then she was relaxed. Hopefully this was a sign she was getting more comfortable with me.

"How long have you had this fascination with pain? Was it always there, or did you become curious somehow?" I ask, it was time to probe a little deeper.

"Well, err I don't know, it's hard to explain." She stammers. She turns her head away, suddenly very interested in the view from the car window.

"Try, and look at me while you do girly." Her head whips around in shock, and I can see the embarrassed flush staining her cheeks.

"Okay, but I don't know how much sense it will make, it doesn't even make sense to me." There is a note of defiance in her tone.

"Let me be the judge of that girly, you might be surprised."

She takes a deep shuddering breath and I wait for her to get the words out.

"Well, I always knew I had a high pain threshold, things that other people found really unbearable I could cope with."

"What things?" I prod.

"Medical procedures, that sort of thing, except the dentist, that scares me silly."

"Most people dislike the dentist Holly." I smile. Myself included.

"It's a bit more than dislike."

"So, come on, how did you move from having a high pain threshold to wanting to explore D/s?"

"I read a lot, romance mainly, and I came across a couple of books with a D/s theme to them. I know it sounds sappy, but they spoke to me." She's blushing again.

"What was it about them that caught your attention?"

"It was the way they got carried away from everything, the way their mind was quiet."

"Lot's of people want a way to switch off, why the fascination with the pain aspect?" I push.

"Does it matter why?"

"Oh yes girly, it matters a lot. I need to know if you really are a masochist, or if you're just a tourist trying it on for size." This relationship wouldn't go much further if that was the case.

"You want to know why?" She snaps. "Okay, here it is then. I dream in pain, I dream of pain so pure and bright that it pushes everything out of me in a huge tidal wave of pain and light, until I am empty of everything except the clear, pure brightness of the pain." She's spitting the words out, like poison from her soul.

Her face is pinched and white and her eyes are rimmed in red and glistening with her angry tears.

"Good answer girly, spoken like a true masochist." I pull up in the restaurant car park and turn to face her properly.

# HOLLY

I can feel the tears hovering about to fall, where had all the words come from? It felt like they had been ripped out of my very soul. I need to get myself back under control before we get out of the car.

"It's okay Holly, it's not wrong to feel like that. Some of us are just so hardwired that we need a bit of extra help to let go." His gaze was gentle and he reaches out to catch a tear before it falls.

"How can you be so nice when you're such a sadist?" I ask in confusion.

"Well, there aren't many of us around you know, we are a select few, the caring sadist." He laughs and I can't help smiling in return.

"I didn't think there were any."

"Just because I enjoy inflicting pain on someone who enjoys it doesn't mean I'm an unfeeling robot, I have feelings too, I can feel deeply for someone, love someone. It adds to the satisfaction I get from giving someone what they need, if I care about them too."

"That makes sense I suppose." Everything was so confusing.

"Good, now let's go eat." He opens the car door and jumps out, before walking around to open my door.

This felt so strange, being on a date with someone from the club, like two worlds colliding. I'd always felt they should stay separate, like the kink world should be kept in the shadows and not cross over to every day life.

Gemma and Elissa had shown me a little bit that it wasn't necessarily like that for everyone. It seemed it wasn't for Bill.

Pulling myself back from my thoughts to find Bill holding a chair out from the table for me, I hurry to sit and get settled.

"You look very deep in thought, are they good thoughts or bad thoughts?"

"They're confused thoughts." I reply with a small smile

"Talk to me, tell me what you are thinking." He stares at me intently

"I never realised people could mix the kink side of their lives with the everyday side of life."

"Not everyone does, for some people the kink is just for the club or the bedroom, but for those of us who want the D/s lifestyle it's hard to switch it off at the bedroom door." He explains.

"I always felt that it was part of a dream world, a fantasy, not real." I'm not explaining myself very well.

"If you get to live your fantasy then you are really lucky. I get to live mine most of the time, I'm a lucky man." He smiles, like a little boy with a big bag of sweets.

"Does it ever truly work like that though? I mean if you are living your fantasy what's left to fantasise about?" I ask.

"Ahh, well that's the good bit, fantasies aren't rationed, you can always imagine more." He replies with a grin.

After a fun, relaxed dinner we arrive at the club just before nine. It's strange to see the main room empty and quiet. It still smells faintly of leather and sex though.

"So what sort of crowd do you get in on a Saturday night then? I've only ever been on a Friday night before."

"Pretty much the same, some people come on both nights, for some it's just more convenient on a weekend." He explains as he begins to flip the switches to turn on all the spot lights on the scene areas.

The play areas look really intimidating lit like that and my gaze keeps drifting to the St Andrews cross.

"Not tonight girly, tonight is a work night." He turns me to face the door to reception and gives me a sharp slap on the arse to get me moving.

The bar staff are the first to arrive, followed by the dungeon monitors, then the first few members begin to drift through the door. I recognise a few faces, some nod and smile, some don't even look at me. There are lots of people I don't know and they are all friendly. There are obviously still people who don't like me because of what Amy did.

"Will you be okay checking people in for a few minutes? I need to go get some stock from the store room for the bar." Bill said after about thirty minutes.

The big rush of people has cleared and now people are drifting through the door in two's and three's I'm sure I can cope one my own for a little while.

"Yes Sir, I'll be fine."

"Good girl, I won't be too long."

He rushes through the door into the main room and I turn to the next couple coming through the door with a smile.

A few minutes later the door opens and my heart sinks as Andrew swaggers in. There isn't anyone else in reception and I resign myself to having to deal with him on my own.

"Well look who we have here, it didn't take you long to get your feet under the table did it?" He sneers.

"Do you have your membership card?" I try to be polite, but I just want to run away and hide.

"What's the rush? Surely you can spare a few minutes for an old play partner." He leans over the desk so his face is right next to mine.

"I need you to sign your entry card." I say pushing the card across the desk at him. If I ignore his comments maybe he'll give up.

"You can ignore me all you like, but we will scene again." His face hardens.

"No, I'm not allowed to play with anyone but Bill, even if I wanted to which I don't." Maybe I just need to be really blunt.

"Well what Bill doesn't know won't hurt him will it?"

"I don't want to scene with you, and if you carry on harassing me I will tell Bill."

"Oh, I don't think you will, who do you think Bill will believe? The well-respected member of the club who is a Dom and a business man or the no one sub who has already been banned from the club once."

My heart sinks, who knows what he lies he could tell Bill, and Bill probably would believe him, after all, he doesn't really know me and what he does know hasn't painted me in a good light.

"I won't play with you." I say firmly.

"You will, or I will tell Bill you came on to me, he won't like that." He grabs my wrist and leans closer to me so that his face is almost touching mine. "I'm sure you can be a little friendlier to me if you really try."

The door opens and Bill comes through into reception. Andrew pulls his hand back and turns to smile at Bill.

"Bill, it's good to see you."

"Andrew, how are you? Do you have a good night lined up?" Bill asks as though they are friends.

If they are friends then Bill would definitely believe Andrew over me, especially if Andrew said the right thing.

"Just here to catch up with a few people, I don't have anyone to play with at the moment." He looks across the desk at me with a grin. "Unless Holly here would like to play again?"

I can feel the heat rise in my face, what do I say now? If I say no will he say anything to Bill?

"I'm sorry Andrew, but Holly won't be playing with anyone but me from now on." Bill says, but he still has a smile on his face, he likes Andrew, he doesn't see any threat from him.

"I'm sorry Bill, I didn't know Holly was off the market."

"That's okay, it's a recent thing so it's not surprising." He shakes Andrews hand again and lets him move past into the main room.

Just as he goes through the door Andrew turns and gives me an evil leer that makes my skin crawl and a shiver travels over me.

## BILL

I turn back to Holly after Andrew has left and her face is flushed red, she isn't looking me in the eye. Something is bothering her, was she just embarrassed that Andrew was someone she played with?

I haven't seen her so flustered since she came back in here to apologise to Elissa.

"Are you okay Holly? Has something upset you?"

Her eyes flit around the room, looking at anything but me. She's hiding something.

"Answer me girly." I snap

Her eyes fly to mine and she looks like a rabbit caught in the headlights.

"I'm sorry Sir, I just didn't know what to say to him. I don't want to play with him again."

"You could have just said that, after all, those are the rules. You don't have to play with anyone Holly, even me." I laugh

"I know what the rules are, I just don't want to make anyone angry." There are tears in her eyes, and I wonder why she's reacting like this.

"Did someone upset you Holly? Did someone not take no for an answer?"

"No, it's nothing like that Sir." The look on her face says it is, but unless she tells me I can't help. If it was someone a while ago, I still can't do much, but it would be good to know.

"Well now you're with me no one should bother you and if they do just send them to me and I will deal with them." I pull her in for a hug and she clings to me like a lifeline. Something really has her rattled.

I pull her head back with her hair and take her mouth in a deep kiss. It doesn't take long to have her moaning with arousal and now her face is flushed for a much more pleasurable reason.

"Now that's a much better look to see on your face. Let's get back to work." I give her a nudge back behind the desk as more people come in through the front door.

It's good to have some company behind the desk and most people seem interested to meet Holly. She seems shy at first, but soon relaxes and begins to chat with people more. By the time the rush has cleared a little it's almost midnight and her eyes are sparkling with pleasure.

"Have you had fun helping me tonight girly?" I ask with a smile.

"I have, it's been fun meeting new people and I've loved watching you work. You know everyone who comes through the door."

"It's my job to know everyone, I need to know what sort of people I let in through the door, otherwise people who really shouldn't be on the scene could come in and no one wants that to happen."

She looks like she is about to say something, but then another couple walk in through the door.

I wish she would trust me enough to tell me what's bothering her, but I suppose that will come in time.

I hope she isn't lying about something, I can't deal with someone else cheating on me. She really doesn't seem the type to do something like that though, at least I don't think she is.

At the end of the night I drive her home and walk her to her door.

"I had fun tonight, thank you." She says quietly.

"Thank you for all your help, it was good to have company on reception." I've only just realised how true that is. I've spent far too much time alone in the last few years.

"When will I see you again?" I can hear the uncertainty in her voice.

"So eager." I laugh.

"I'm sorry, it's okay, don't worry about it." She turns away, head down and moves to unlock her door.

"Hey! Stop, I was kidding, I want to see you again Holly." I pull her back around and into my arms. She is so defensive and stiff.

"You don't have to be nice you know, you've given me more than I ever imagined was out there, it's okay if you don't want to carry on."

"I want to carry on Holly, never doubt that." I say lifting her chin and looking her in the eye. "I don't do things just to be nice, if I didn't want to be with you I would tell you."

"Are you sure? I'm not much of a catch you know."

"I have eyes Holly, I see who you are, does this feel like I'm just being nice?" I grab her hand and press it hard against my erection.

Her pupils dilate with desire and I hear her gasp.

"No Sir." She whispers.

"So, we will have no more silly talk about me just being nice."

"No Sir."

"Okay, now off to bed with you and I will call you tomorrow." I kiss her gently and push her towards the door.

"Goodnight Sir." She smiles as she closes the front door, leaving me on the garden path like a love-struck teenager.

# HOLLY

My smile fades once the door is closed and I'm alone. What am I going to do? Andrew isn't going to stop trying to get me to play, his threats are beginning to scare me, and I have a feeling they are only going to get worse. Would Bill believe me if I tell him what Andrew is doing? He's already told me he won't tolerate lying, and he's known Andrew much longer than he's known me.

Maybe I can just keep away from Andrew, never let myself be alone with him. If I always stay with Bill or Gemma and Elissa then he can't threaten me. I don't want to cause any more trouble at the club, people are still wary of me as it is, if I cause trouble between Bill and Andrew they will just assume I am the trouble maker.

I don't need to be friends with everyone, but I've started to realise just how much I want to be able to go to the club. Bill has shown me that I can find what I was looking for and I can't turn my back on it now.

My mind made up, and my determination restored I head off to bed. A relaxing Sunday is just what I need, no plans, just relaxation.

I wake to the sun flooding through the open curtains, I must have forgotten to close them last night. For some reason I feel upset by this small trivial thing. I'm still tired and I ache everywhere. My empty room feels so lonely, I'm so alone. The tears come suddenly and unexpected, running down my face to drip off my chin wetting the sheet.

What's wrong with me? I have no reason to be upset, I give myself a mental shake and get out of bed, a shower will make me feel better I'm sure. I still can't shake my lethargy as I eat my toast and drink my coffee. Maybe I'm coming down with something, I might have a nap later.

I wander listlessly around the house, picking up a book only to put it down after reading the same sentence several times without taking in a word, turning on the tv and switching channels with no idea what I'm watching. After a couple of hours, I give up and go back to bed.

My phone wakes me a couple of hours later, oh Bill said he would ring me today, I grab the phone excited to hear his voice.

"Hello." Even I can here the excitement in my voice.

"Hey Holly." It's Gemma.

"Oh, hi Gemma, how are you?"

"Am I that bad, or were you expecting someone else?" she laughs. Oh, to be that confident.

"Sorry Gemma, I'm not feeling too great today."

"Aw honey, what's wrong?"

"I really don't know, I feel so tired and achy and for some reason really emotional. Maybe I'm getting the flu."

"Do you have a temperature?" she asks.

"No nothing like that, not yet anyway."

"You aren't ill sweetie, you are dropping." She says gently.

"What does that mean? Dropping?"

"You played really hard on Friday, it looked really intense, did you play more when you went through to Bill's place?"

"Well yes, that was even more intense to be honest." I smile at the memory of it, and even more tears fill my eyes.

"You have sub drop!" she says, like I should know what that is.

"What is sub drop?"

"When we play it releases lots of chemicals into our body, that's why it feels so good, but when those chemicals start to wear off we feel the drop from the high. It can happen right away or a few days later. It's never nice." I hear the sympathy in her voice.

"Will it go away?"

"It will, but you need to be kind to yourself for a couple of days. Are you seeing Bill today?"

"I don't know, he said he would call me today."

"Call him and tell him, he needs to know."

"I shouldn't bother him, he's probably busy."

"This is the sort of thing you need to be telling him, he needs to know so he can help, it's called aftercare, you've heard of that right?" She has a bossy tone no submissive should ever have.

"I will tell him when he rings." I promise.

"Make sure you do." She insists.

"I will." I laugh. "What did you want anyway?"

"Oh, yes I was just ringing to see what you were up to today, Elissa and I were thinking of getting together for coffee and cake and we thought you might like to join us."

"That would be great."

"Now I've spoken to you though I think we need bigger plans. What's your address?"

I give her my address automatically.

"Fabulous, we'll be there in an hour." She says and the phone goes dead.

I look over at the mirror on the dresser and wince at the view. My hair is a bird nest from going to bed while it was still wet. I jump out of bed and attack the mess with the hair brush. I've just finished getting dressed when I hear the doorbell.

Opening the door, I find a sympathetic Gemma and Elissa, both their arms filled with shopping bags.

"Let us in, we have every snack food known to woman kind in these bags." Gemma steps past me followed more slowly by Elissa.

"You didn't have to come over." I say with a grateful smile in Elissa's direction.

"Yes, we did, we both know what subdrop feels like. You need snack food, hugs and maybe a Disney movie or two." She says following Gemma into the kitchen.

"Chocolate or Ice cream?" Gemma says from the kitchen doorway, holding one up in each hand.

"Mulan or Tangled?" Elissa asks holding up a DVD in each hand.

I look at them both and I'm so touched I just burst into tears all over again.

# BILL

Sundays are the only day the club is closed, it's my day to clean and check all the equipment and restock the bar. I've always found it relaxing to be in here on my own, the quiet is so different to an open night. I like to plan scenes while I'm cleaning the equipment, I can picture a submissive in different positions and predicaments. Now the only person I'm picturing in Holly, every scene I plan is for her.

It had been good spending time with her last night too, I enjoyed chatting with her. The more time we spend together the more relaxed she's getting. Although she had seemed anxious again at one-point last night. I will get to the bottom of why if it keeps happening.

I need to ring her soon, check how she's doing and arrange to see her again. I want to see her more than just Friday nights in here, I want to see her outside the scene too. I want to fall asleep with her sated in my arms and wake in the morning with her draped across my chest.

Good grief I'm getting positively sappy in my old age. The door bell rings announcing the arrival of the drinks delivery, time to get back to work. It isn't long till I have the bar stocked and the club cleaned and ready for opening.

Heading through the door to my home, I pull out my phone a dial Holly's number.

"Hello." Her voice sounds odd.

"Hello girly, what's wrong?" I'm instantly alert, something isn't right.

"Nothing, I'm fine." She whispers.

"No, you aren't, you need to tell him Holly." I can hear Gemma's voice in the background.

"Tell me what Holly? What's going on."

"I'm okay really, I'm just feeling a bit low. Gemma and Elissa say I have sub drop, but I'm okay honestly." I can hear the tears in her voice.

"Put Gemma on the phone." I demand.

"Good afternoon Bill, how are you?" Gemma's asks sweetly.

"How is she?" I snap.

"She's down, weepy, but we've brought ice cream and chocolate and Disney films, she'll be fine."

"Do I need to come over right now?" It sounds like Gemma and Elissa have things covered and sometimes a bit of girly time is exactly what's needed.

"No, she'll be fine until later, we're keeping her company, but I think she might need hugs from her Sir later."

"Thank you, Gemma, and thank Elissa for me."

"I will do, don't worry we'll take care of her." She reassures me.

"Put Holly back on the phone."

"Hello."

"Holly, you should have phoned me and told me you weren't feeling good. I need to know these things from you, not Gemma."

"I'm sorry Sir." She sounds lost. "I didn't know what it was, I just felt lonely this morning and I kept crying, it's so pathetic."

"It is not pathetic, it's perfectly normal, although that still doesn't make it easy to cope with. You had a lot of endorphins and adrenalin rushing round your system, that takes some getting over." I reassure her.

"I suppose so." She mumbles.

"I know so, now relax and enjoy your time with Gemma and Elissa and I'll be round to see you later. Do you like Chinese food?"

"I don't want to be any trouble if you're busy."

"I'm never too busy for proper aftercare Holly, I'll be round later with dinner."

"Yes Sir, I'll see you later then."

"Good girl, now go relax and be good to yourself."

"Bye." She whispers.

"Bye holly." I hang up the phone and head out to do some shopping before I go to Holly's later.

## HOLLY

By the time Gemma and Elissa leave I am feeling a little bit better. Who knew a bit of chocolate and a Disney film could make so much difference. It's been years since I watched any Disney and I'm a bit embarrassed at how much I enjoyed it.

The fact that Gemma and Elissa have been so lovely has helped lots too, that and hearing from Bill. I really need a hug from him, hopefully he will oblige when he comes over later. I look down at myself with growing horror, I look an absolute mess. My hair is a mess again and I'm wearing sloppy sweat pants and big chunky socks.

I rush to the bathroom and jump in the shower. I can't have Bill seeing me like this, he would run in the other direction as soon as I open the front door. I'm more than a little embarrassed at how pathetic I was this morning, maybe I wasn't really cut out for all this. If it affects me this much could it really be for me?

The thought of turning my back on it all makes me feel sad and down all over again. Although that's what I had been about to do after I'd apologised Elissa. Until Bill had shown me what it was really like, I'd thought it would be easy to walk away. Now the thought filled me with dread.

I pull on some comfortable lounge pants and a loose top and tie my hair up in a simple knot. I'm just coming back down the stairs when there is a knock at the door. I rush to answer it and find a smiling Bill on the doorstep holding up a takeout bag. I fling my arms around him and hold on tight, feeling the tears start to flow once again.

"Hey hey, it's okay girly, you're okay." He says softly rubbing my back with his free hand.

"I'm sorry." I mumble into his shirt.

"You have nothing to be sorry about." He kisses my head and holds me tighter.

"But, I'm being really pathetic." I sob.

"Stop now. You are not being pathetic, you are being human and it's perfectly normal."

"Really? Will this happen every time? Should I not scene anymore?" I ask confused.

"It might not happen every time, or it will get less and less as we go on. Now go get some plates and let's eat."

I lead him into the kitchen and grab some plates from the cupboard, I put them on the table and turn to get some cutlery from the drawer. Bill is already opening carton after carton of Chinese food.

"That's a lot of food, are we expecting guests?" I ask with a grin.

"I'm hungry." He says defensively. "Plus, I didn't know what you liked so I got a variety."

I sit at the table and peak in all the boxes, he isn't joking when he says he got a variety, there is so much food.

"We'll be eating this for a week, we'll be having left overs for lunch, dinner and breakfast at this rate."

"No, I eat a lot, I tend to burn up lots of energy when I'm flogging little masochists." He winks at me with a cheeky grin.

It's still strange to think of this cheeky happy Bill as the Sadist I now know him to be.

"So, tell me about today? How did you feel? How do you feel now?" Suddenly he's serious again.

"I just felt really sad, weepy and sad, and incredibly lonely." I might as well be honest with him, he seemed to almost expect this to happen.

"It sounds like typical sub drop to me. It tends to highlight all the things you aren't happy with and makes you really emotional."

"How do people cope with it? It's really not nice at all." I ask.

"People find what helps them best, cuddles, support, chocolate, company, space to be on their own, whatever helps them best. You'll find what works for you, and it does happen less the more you play." He explains.

"The chocolate did help lots, and the girly time, your hugs helped too." I say shyly.

"I'm glad it helped, and there's plenty more where they came from, they aren't rationed."

We eat in a comfortable silence, and then he helps me with the dishes. Once I've set the coffee brewing we move into the lounge and sit next to each other on the sofa.

"So, how was your day? What have you been up to?"

"I've been at the club, cleaning and stocking up the bar."

"How long have you been managing the club? How did you end up doing it?" I'm curious, it's not the kind of job you see advertised at the job centre after all.

"I was a member at the club, I always loved spending time there. When the owner and his wife had their first child they decided that the club life wasn't practical any longer. He didn't want to sell the club though, it brings in a good income, so they were looking for a manager. The restaurant I was manager of was being sold and the new owner wanted to manage it himself, so I needed a new job. The two things coincided."

"How long ago was that?"

"Almost six years now, and I've never looked back. I really love my job."

"What do you love so much about it?"

"Lots of things, but I suppose the main thing is I love giving people a safe place just to be themselves. The chance to explore who they want to be, to find their fantasies." I can see his passion.

"That is a very magical job." I smile at him.

# BILL

She's bringing out my poetic side again. I will be losing my reputation as a jokey sadist if I carry on. People are going to get the idea I'm a big softy.

"Of course, one of the other things I love about my job, is I get the chance to inflict pain on little masochistic subs."

"You don't fool me, I know you're all mushy on the inside." She winks cheekily at me from the other end of the sofa.

"Oh really! Be careful girly, you don't want to be getting into trouble now do you?"

"Oh no, never." She shakes her head, but I can see her smile.

"So, tell me, what do you do for work?" I don't really know enough about her, it was time to fix that.

"I have probably the most boring job in the world, I work in a call centre. I just process calls all day, I even have a script to follow."

"Every job has it's merits."

"Well about the only one I can see to this one is that it pays the bills and keeps a roof over my head. At some point I might get promoted to supervisor, but that's about it really."

"Have you never thought of doing something else?" I ask.

"I have, but I have no idea what I would do. I'm not skilled for anything really."

"What did you want to be when you were a little girl?" Everyone has a dream job when they're small.

"I really wanted to be a hairdresser or a vet, but then I realised vets didn't just get to cuddle kittens and puppies all day, they actually had to stick their hands up cow's bottoms." She laughs.

"That's enough to put anyone off really." I agree.

"Definitely! I soon went off that idea. I did have a Saturday job in a hairdressers when I was a teenager, but it was quite boring."

"If you could do any job in the world what would you do?"

"I have no idea, what did you want to be when you were a cute little boy?" She winks at me.

"Oh, I wanted to be what every little boy wants to be, an Astronaut." I laugh.

"So, what do you want to do tonight Sir?"

"I think a cosy snuggle on your very comfy sofa and a film sounds like an excellent idea, don't you? Definitely no Disney films though." I scowl.

She laughs loudly and gets up to open a cupboard next to the Tv.

"How about a comedy then?" she asks.

"That will do nicely girly, what do you have?"

We debate for a while, but eventually settle on an action comedy film. I pull her closer to me on the sofa and she wriggles in against me, her head resting on my chest as the movie starts.

It's been a long time since I just sat and watched a film with someone. I don't think I ever did this with Hannah, she always wanted to be doing something, going out somewhere, she was a party girl at heart really, maybe that's why she had cheated on me, maybe I was too boring.

I can't change who I am though, not that I want to, I'm happy with the man I am, happy in my own skin and my own life. If I could keep Holly in my life I think I would be one of the happiest people on earth. She compliments me, her shyness is being replaced by what I think is her natural sass and I love it, my natural humour will always be amused by her cheekiness, so long as it didn't get out of hand.

I wouldn't do her any favours in this lifestyle if I let her get away with too much bratting. A bit of brat is okay though, it gives me an excuse to punish her with my cane. As we sit snuggling my mind drifts, wondering exactly how deep we can go into the S/m side of our relationship. The D/s side was easier to gage, I am Dominant and she is submissive and from what I can see we are both even in now far we want that to go. Not twenty-four seven, but definitely further than the inside of the bedroom.

The Sadism/ masochism side of things is harder to gage. It's only by pushing each other that we will find our limits. I have an idea that we have much further to go yet before either of us get close to our limits. The thought of exploring with her excites me more than anything has for years.

## HOLLY

I'm so relaxed snuggling next to Bill watching the film. It feels so good having someone to share my evening, someone to talk to. My life has been lonely for too long, I have work colleagues, but once I'm home and I shut the door it's just me, on my own in the silence of my house. Sometimes the silence was deafening, it shouted to me that I was alone, that no one loved me.

My parents are gone, both of them dying of different forms of cancer within a couple of years of each other, I was their only child. Sometimes apart from the people who rang the call centre I could go for days without speaking to anyone. I had enjoyed the conversation just as much as I was enjoying the closeness now.

Was that why I was feeling such a strong pull to be with Bill? Was I just so desperate for someone to be with that I'd jumped at the first person to ask? No that can't be it or I would have taken Andrew up on his offer the first time we played. A shudder runs through me at the thought of Andrew. He really was scary, I don't know what sort of thing he might accuse me of if I carry on refusing him.

"Are you okay Holly?" Bill murmurs into my hair.

"Yes, why?"

"You shivered, are you cold?"

"No, I'm fine, I feel lots better than I did this morning." I realise just how true that is, this morning I had felt desolate and alone, now I was relaxed and calm.

"Well as soon as the film ends it's off to bed for you, you need your rest." He pulls me closer against his chest.

"It's still early, I'm not a child you know."

"No, you aren't a child, but you are my submissive, which means you do as you are told when it comes to your health and safety." He says firmly.

"I told you I feel fine now." I snap.

"Yes, you did, but if you want to carry on feeling fine you will go to bed early. I know how sub drop works much better than you do at the moment and trust me you will feel it again tomorrow if you don't get enough sleep tonight. You need to be able to go to work in the morning, don't you?"

"Yes, I do. I suppose you're right." I mumble grudgingly.

"Yes girly, I know how annoying it is when your Dom is always right." He laughs.

"Hmph!"

"Now don't sulk, it's really not a good look." He ruffles my hair, which just irritates me even more. "Now pay attention to the film."

"Yes Sir." I relax against him again, and by the time the credits are rolling my eyes are drooping tiredly. Dammit he was right, suddenly I'm exhausted.

"Come on girly, lets get you tucked up in bed." He pulls me up from the sofa and follows me into the bedroom.

"I can manage to get ready for bed you know."

"I know you can, but I can't hold you close all night if I go home, now can I?" He says with twinkle in his eye.

He pulls his shirt off and I'm mesmerised by his naked chest, I have a desperate urge to run my hands over the planes and hollows of his body. I can't tear my eyes away from the sculpted muscles of his shoulders and arms.

"Focus Holly, you need to get ready for bed." I can hear the laughter in his voice.

I go through to the bathroom to brush my teeth and when I come out he is standing in just his boxer shorts. I pull a night shirt from the dresser and pull my top off, I'm just unhooking my bra when he snatches the night shirt from the bed.

"You won't be needing that girly, I like to feel warm skin next to mine, if I'm sharing a bed I want the full experience."

Okay, well I can't deny that I will enjoy feeling his chest all hot and naked next to me all night. I had slept really well when I stayed at his house, but then we had just scened. It felt different just getting undressed after watching a film.

I take the plunge and push my pants down and off, then I dive under the covers. His laughter trails after me.

"You can run girly, but you can't hide." He says and yanks the duvet off me.

"Nooooo! it's too cold." I yelp.

"You'll soon warm up when I get in too." He slaps my arse and walks into the bathroom whistling.

I shiver and reach for the duvet.

"Leave it!" His voice booms from the bathroom and I snatch my hand back. How did he know?

He comes out of the bathroom with a smile on his face and climbs on the bed pulling the duvet behind him like a super hero cape. He's such a joker, he comes to rest lying over my body and the heat radiating off him warms me instantly.

"Now girly, it's time to sleep, so tuck yourself just here, in this special spot just made for you and rest." He rolls off me and pulls me close so my head is resting in the hollow of his shoulder.

I feel a huge sigh escape as I relax against him. An overwhelming sense of belonging sweeps through me. I could lie here forever and never want to move. I can hear his heart beating against my ear and the soothing rhythm sends me to sleep.

# BILL

I can hear her breathing deepen as she relaxes into me more. She makes a cute little snorting noise as she drifts off to sleep. I relax back into the softness of the bed with contentment. Could there be any better feeling than holding a warm woman who trusts you enough to fall asleep in the same bed as you?

I hope she is feeling less droppy tomorrow, I know it can't be easy to go to work when you are suffering. She had so obviously needed my hugs earlier, but she hadn't been demanding or clingy. She was trying to cause as little trouble as possible. She has obviously had to rely on herself all the time, she needs to try and lean on me a little.

I settle down to sleep with a smile on my face and a warm contented woman in my arms.

I wake in the morning to find her draped across my chest, her leg thrown over mine, pinning me to the bed. I run my hand down her back and grab a handful of her peachy arse. She shifts in her sleep and I grip harder to prevent her escape. She mumbles and shifts against me; my cock stirs against her thigh.

I run my fingers between her legs and brush against her hot pussy. She moves towards my teasing fingers and I slip one inside. Her hot breath brushes my chest as she groans, she squirms on top of me in her sleep and I wonder how long it's going to take her to wake up. I rub my thumb over her clit and thrust my finger deep into her pussy. She is getting wetter and her breathing is becoming shallower and faster.

I look at her face and her cheeks are still pink from sleep, but possibly from unconscious desire too. I press down firmly on her clit and suddenly her eyes pop open.

"Good morning girly." I pull her head down to kiss her. She tries to turn her head away from me, but I yank it back.

"Sir, please. I haven't brushed my teeth." She tries again to turn away.

"I don't care, neither have I. Does my breath smell?" I ask.

"No Sir, not at all." She looks shocked.

"Then neither does yours, now kiss me." I demand.

She brushes her mouth over mine so gently it feels like a feather. I poke my tongue out and tease the crease of her lips.

"Kiss me like you mean it girly, we aren't playing at this." I pull her head back down to mine and she plunges her tongue between my lips to explore my mouth.

I move my fingers slowly in and out of her pussy and feel her wetness, she's very aroused now she is totally awake. She wriggles and squirms against my fingers and a groan escapes her.

"That feels so good Sir." She mumbles.

I want to sink into her heat, let her set me on fire.

"Take me inside Holly." She lifts her head to look at me in surprise.

"What? You mean, me on top?"

"That's exactly what I mean, now, up you go." I push her up to straggle my hips, putting her wet heat right over my throbbing cock.

"But Sir, I've never, you know."

"You're so cute when you blush. Just do what feels good, if it feels good for you it probably will for me." I let my hands rest gently on her waist and wait to see what she will do next.

She looks at me shyly from under her lashes. I raise my eye brow and she moves tentatively against me. Her pupils dilate as her desire flames and she moves more forcefully against my cock.

"You feel so good." She gasps.

"Put my cock in your pussy Holly, fill yourself with me." I guide her hand to my cock and wrap her fingers around my hardness.

Her hand moves slowly up the length of me and her thumb brushes over the tip, then her hand plunges back down to the base to squeeze firmly. I groan as her caresses become bolder, she was torturing me, keeping me waiting.

## HOLLY

His cock is hot and hard in my hand and I feel a sense of power as I make him groan. His cock feels like steel wrapped in silk, and the heat radiates through my hand. I pull his cock towards my pussy and rub the head against my clit. Tingles run through me at the teasing contact.

"Holly please." His voice is hoarse with desire.

I'm really unsure of what he wants me to do, every encounter we have had so far, he has been firmly in charge. This feels more like I'm in charge, I'm totally out of my comfort zone, and definitely out of my league experience wise.

"Sir, I'm not sure I can do this, it feels odd."

"Why does it feel odd?" Now this feels even stranger, having a conversation while we're having sex.

"Because you are always in charge, you are my Sir." The rush of feeling I get from actually saying those words out loud is heady indeed.

"If it makes it easier I am ordering you to take my cock and fill your pussy with it." His smile is sinfully sexy.

His words turn me on even more and I can feel a rush of moisture coat my thighs. I lift myself up off his thighs and pull his cock towards me. I lodge the tip of his cock just inside my pussy, I look down into his eyes as I wait hovering above him.

His face is flushed and his breathing is harsh, I can see he is just keeping control, trying not to move, letting me control what happens. I don't understand why though, he is a Dominant man, I thought he would always be in control.

The need to move grows the longer I wait, my thighs begin to burn with the strain of holding up my weight. Still I wait though, I don't know what I'm waiting for. We both want me to move but some instinct is telling me to wait just a little bit longer.

"Holly!" his voice carries a warning, he's reaching his limit.

I feel the power radiate through me, I have this big gorgeous man at my mercy and I feel amazing. I move slightly and his cock moves to press against my clit. The head of his cock is slick from my pussy and the slide of skin against skin feels decadent.

His grip on my waist tightens and he groans. I look down at him as I shift and slowly take his length inside. The wait was worth it, the slide of his hardness feels so sexy. I pull back up and let myself drop down to engulf the whole length of him.

I move up and down driving us both to the brink of climax, but I can't seem to push us over.

"Sir, I can't." I wail

"You can girly, do it, send us both." He growls.

I move faster and harder, sweat is slicking my body now and I feel like I am reaching for the moon. The harder I reach for it though the further away it seems to move. In desperation I move my fingers to rub against my clit, so with each downward stroke the pressure increases.

Just a little bit more and I will fly.

"Now Holly, come now." His command triggers the first trembles of my orgasm and I see his face contort as his cock begins to pulse deep inside me.

As my orgasm fades I slump down across his chest with a sigh of contentment. His hands caress my back in long soothing strokes and I melt further into him. I have no idea how long I lie there prone on top of him, but thoughts soon begin to niggle at my brain.

Why had he done that? He had given up all control and put me in charge, why?

"I can practically hear you thinking girly, what's going on in that head of yours?" He asks.

"Why did you do that? I'm confused."

"Do what girly?"

"You gave me all the control, you put me in charge, why?"

"I did it for two reasons Holly, first because nothing builds your confidence like seeing how much you can turn someone on. Second because now you know exactly what you are giving me when you submit to me. Now you know what it feels like to be really in control, and now you have a deeper sense of submission when you hand over that control." He explains.

"Oh, okay."

"Did you like being in charge?"

"For a minute or two I felt really powerful."

"I sense a but coming." He says.

"I don't want to be in charge." I whisper.

"I know you don't girly. Do you have any idea how hard it was for me to lie still and let you be in charge?" He strokes my cheek gently.

"Please don't do it again." I laugh.

Suddenly he flips us over so I am pinned beneath him, his cock is still imbedded in my pussy.

"Don't worry girly, it won't be happening again." He growls.

He proceeds to show me exactly who is in charge.


When I arrive at work I'm only just on time, but I have a smile on my face and a skip in my step. That all changes an hour later when I look up from my desk to see my boss, Jackson, speaking to Andrew in reception. What is he doing here? They go into Jacksons office and the door closes.

I don't know what Andrew does for a living, but I can't think why he would need to visit an energy company call centre. Thirty minutes later the door opens and Andrew walks out, he looks around the office and he smiles when he sees me.

Oh God, what has he just done? How did he even know where I work?

Ten minutes after Andrew has left Jackson calls me into his office. Oh well, I didn't really enjoy this job anyway.

"Holly, how are you today?" Jackson smiles at me as I sit across the desk from him.

"I'm fine thank you." I reply cautiously.

"I just had a visit from someone who knows you, I have to say that the visit unnerved me greatly."

"Really? In what way?"

"He came to tell me about your erm unusual activities at a club in Town at the weekend."

Jackson is blushing, it would be cute if it was for any other reason. I can't believe Andrew outed me, it's the cardinal rule of the scene, NEVER out someone, ever.

"What I do at the weekend has nothing to do with my work here, it's no one's business but mine." I say defensively.

"I quite agree Holly, I told him as much too." I look up in surprise.

"You did?" I squeak.

"Holly whatever you get up to outside of work is entirely your own choice, what worries me though is that this man thought it was acceptable to try to get you in trouble at work."

"I'm sorry he involved you." I truly am, Jackson was a good man, a decent boss.

"Do you want me to phone the police? You could get him charged."

"What with? All he did was tell you something about me, which is actually true. I can't even say it's slander."

"I suppose, is there anyone you can talk to about this at the club you go to? Isn't there supposed to be a community of sorts?" So, he wasn't totally ignorant of the lifestyle then.

Bill's face pops into my mind, I should tell him about this. Outing is a very serious thing, Andrew could ruin someone's life doing what he had just done to me. I can't tell him though, Andrews threat to tell Bill lies about me hangs in the way of that. I could maybe talk to Gemma and Elissa about it though, but would they tell their Sirs?

"So, what happens now?" I ask.

"Absolutely nothing. I have been and continue to be very happy with your work, that is the only thing I need to know about." He smiles.

"Thank you."

"Holly, I do just want to say one more thing. The last couple of weeks you have seemed much happier, you always seemed very lonely before. If this club has done that then I think it's a good thing."

"It is a good thing, and a good man." I smile blushing.

"Then I'm happy for you." He says gesturing to the door.

# BILL

The queue at reception is long tonight, we are never usually this busy on a weekday. I could do with an extra pair of hands on the desk. It's a shame Holly isn't coming in tonight, she had been a huge help last week.

I look up to greet the next person in line and see it's Andrew.

"Hey, how are you doing? We don't normally see you on a week night. Did you have a good time on Saturday night?"

"I did, lots of good people in. It was a good night." He smiles.

"Did you find someone to scene with?" I know Andrew is single.

"No, unfortunately. I'll just have to keep searching."

"I'm sure you'll find the right person. Just relax and let things happen in their own time." I've always thought Andrew was a good chap.

"Holly looked amazing at the weekend." He smiles.

"Look in a different place Andrew, Holly is mine." I stare at him intently.

"Oh of course, I wouldn't dream of encroaching on your territory. I'm just saying she looked good. I had a good time when we scened before." He smiles, but something about his words seems off.

"I get the impression that Holly didn't feel the connection in your scene."

His face hardens slightly, but he seems to realise and schools his features into his usual pleasant smile.

"Sometimes it's there and sometimes it's not, you can never tell." He signs his card and walks through the door into the club.

Something niggles at the back of my mind; my alarm bells are ringing quietly. I can't quite put my finger on why though. Nothing he had just said was out of order really, it was just a vibe he was giving off. I think I need to keep a closer eye on Andrew.

Part of my job was ensuring the safety of the club members, if something isn't right I need to know about it and fix it.

Once the rush dies down, I get someone to cover the desk for a while and I head into the main room to see what's happening. All the scene areas are being used and the room is full of the sounds of pleasure and pain, just as it should be. I move around the room, stopping to chat to several people, everyone is in a good mood, this is why I love my job.

As the evening goes on I find myself searching the room to observe Andrew, he is chatting with a big group of people, all of them seem to be enjoying themselves. There are several unattached submissives in the group and although he is sometimes in conversation with one or another of them he doesn't seem to be singling any one in particular out.

They are all relaxed and smiling too, so he isn't making anyone uncomfortable. Maybe I'm sensing something that isn't there, I've never heard any complaints or negative comments about Andrew. The niggle is still there though and I have learned to trust my gut when it comes to judging people. I might just keep an eye on him for the next few weeks.

Much later when I'm finally lying in my bed, my thoughts drift to Holly. I had enjoyed having her warm body curled up against mine in bed all night, my bed seemed cold and empty tonight. I was getting in so deep, she stirred all my Dominant tendencies as well as my Sadistic ones.

My feelings for her were growing every day, she had impressed me with her bravery when she had come back into the club, and nothing had changed my opinion. She was a strong woman who seems to have had to stand on her own two feet for far too long. She carried a lonely air about her that I really want to chase away. She shouldn't be lonely, she should be cared for and loved, and made to laugh every day.

With her I could relax and let my Sadist out to play, she wouldn't just tolerate the pain she would revel in it. She was the other side of the coin from me, masochist to my Sadist, submissive to my Dominant. I have seen flashes of her sense of humour too, we will never be bored in each other's company.

Suddenly I am imagining the future, our future together. I feel as though we are on the cusp of something life changing. All I want to do is grab her hand and launch us both into the future together.

## HOLLY

I really can't wait to get to the club, due to one thing or another I haven't managed to see Bill since Monday morning. We have spoken on the phone every day though, long conversations when the desk is quiet at the club. Sharing our days with each other and learning more about each other. Somehow it had seemed easier to talk about my life when I'm not being distracted by his overwhelming personality.

Tonight, I am ready to be overwhelmed, the need to feel the rush of pain has been building since the middle of the week, until now it feels like my whole body is itching and at war with itself. Before I scened with Bill it was a curiosity, but it feels as though he opened a door with that first scene and allowed my need to escape. Tonight, that need is running a rampage through my body and only Bill can calm it enough to get it back in the room inside me.

How long this mystery room has been there deep inside me or how it got there I have no idea. Where this need for pain comes from I have no idea. Does this make me a weirdo? Does every masochist feel like this?

I want him to take me further and deeper, but that scares me too. Not the pain or the feeling, but the not knowing exactly how deep this need goes, how far is too far? I'm scared of myself, of what I might need, of how far I might go.

One thought calms me though, and stills my panic a little, Bill will keep me safe. That is the one thing I am sure of. Then I hear the little voice in my head saying he can't protect me if he doesn't know there is something to protect me from. If I don't tell him about Andrew how can he help me?

Maybe when he knows me better and time has moved on more from the Amy incident, maybe then I can tell him and he will believe me over Andrew. At the moment though he would believe Andrew, who he has known much longer than me, especially as Andrew could say anything.

I'm not going to let the shadow of Andrew spoil my night though, I need the release I know the pain can give me too much.

As I get out of my car at the club I see Adam and Elissa just parking up, so I wait for them to get their toy bag and walk over to say hello.

"Hello Holly, how are you this evening?" Adam smiles at me.

"I'm okay thank you, how are you?"

"You look more than okay Holly, you are positively vibrating with energy." He laughs.

"I'm just ready to play." I blush.

"Hey Holly, you look gorgeous, I love your corset." Elissa leans in to give me a hug.

I hug her back and find unexpected tears pricking my eyes. I hadn't really had any friends before, I was so touched that Elissa and Gemma seem to want to be my friend. These two women who had every reason not to like me had actively sought me out and befriended me. I felt honoured by their friendship.

As we turn towards the door of the club another car pulls into the car park. I stiffen as I see it's Andrew. Now I am going to be on edge all night, waiting for him to say something. He smiles at me as he reaches us, it makes my skin crawl.

"Hey Adam, good to see you. Hello Elissa, you are looking beautiful as always."

"Good to see you too Andrew, how's work?" Adam shakes his hand with a smile, but I can see Elissa isn't impressed with his compliments.

"Work is good, very busy though." Andrew says, then he turns towards me. "How are you this evening Holly? How was your work this week?" he has a sly smile on his face and I stiffen in shock that he would be stupid enough to ask me that after what he did.

Surely at this point I am more of a threat to him than he is to me. If I tell Bill what he did he would be barred from the club, he would lose his friends. Maybe he didn't care, or maybe he is so sure I won't say anything because of his threats.

"Work has been really good this week thank you. I had some amazing feedback from my boss on Monday." I tell him defiantly.

His face loses its smug grin and hardens in anger, I flinch and take a step back away from him.

"Are you okay Holly?" Adam asks with concern. He can't see Andrews face, he just saw my reaction.

"I'm fine Adam, but I should get inside, Bill will be waiting." I give him a shaky smile, Elissa's eyes narrow on me as I turn and enter the club.

I take a deep cleansing breath as I push open the door and I have a smile in pace as I walk up to the desk and into Bill's arms.

# BILL

There she is! My girl, she looks gorgeous as she rushes into reception and right into my arms. This week has been way too long without her. Her arms wrap tightly around me and she holds me tighter when I pull back a little.

"Is everything okay Holly?" I look down into her face.

"Yes Sir, I just missed you this week." She says into my shoulder.

"Well I missed you too girly, are you ready to play tonight?" I laugh.

"Yes, please Sir. I need to." She says with desperation in her voice.

"Are you sure everything is okay Holly, you can tell me anything you should know that." I reassure her.

Again, I get the feeling that she is holding something back from me. Does she not trust me enough to look after her? I pull her in tighter and she rests her head in the hollow of my shoulder, igniting all my protective instincts.

Hearing the door, I look up to see Adam and Elissa walking in. Elissa is looking at Holly with concern, something is definitely going on with my submissive and I need to find out what. She pulls back from me and moves behind the desk, busying herself with the box of membership cards.

The door opens again and Andrew walks in, they must have all arrived at the same time. My gut tells me Andrew has something to do with my skittish sub. I turn a questioning look on Adam and he shrugs, hopefully I will get the chance to talk to him later. If something happened in the car park he would have seen it.

For the moment though the desk was too busy for me to leave.

"Adam could I ask you to look after Holly for me until the desk quietens down a bit more?"

"Of course, Bill, it will be my pleasure, Holly can spend some time chatting with Elissa."

"Well Leo and Gemma are already inside, so the girls can chat together maybe."

"They will have fun until we need them for something interesting." Adam laughs and taking Elissa's arm he holds his other arm out for Holly to take.

"Go in with Adam Girly I will be in as soon as I can." I kiss her deeply and send her off with her friend.

Turning I move to the desk to book Andrew in.

"Have a good night Andrew, I hope you find someone to play with." I say, watching him closely.

"Me too, but I will enjoy chatting and watching the scenes if I don't." He says with a smile and walks through the door to the main room.

He really hasn't done anything that I can see, maybe I am just being paranoid.

Holly had seemed really ready to play, like she needed the release, well that I could help her with. As I book people in for their own fun I mentally plan what scene I want to give her. If she is so desperate for a release I should start hard and push her a bit more. A gentle build up won't overwhelm her thoughts if she is struggling to switch off.

Maybe my canes need to come out tonight, the sting will overwhelm her senses and allow her to turn off her thoughts. Yes, definitely canes for her tonight.

I will let her have her catch up with Gemma and Elissa, that will help her relax enough so that I can push her far enough to let go.

I check each person in with a growing sense of excitement, I have missed her this week. Henry who usually manages the club for me a couple of days each week had called in sick on Monday night. He had sounded shocking to be fair. He also had his day job to keep up with, he only managed the club on a volunteer basis, mainly because he loved the scene.

I had enjoyed speaking to Holly every night though, I feel like this week has given me a better understanding of who she is. We had talked about work, hobbies, and family. She had told me about her parents and how they had died. She really had been alone for quite a while.

Well she isn't alone any more. I have no intention of letting her go.

## HOLLY

I'm enveloped in a hug as soon as we reach Leo and Gemma, they are sitting in their usual spot further away from the dance floor so it's easier to talk. The fact that this also gives them a better view of the play areas is an added bonus.

Adam and Leo sit on one sofa and Gemma pulls myself and Elissa over to the far end of the other sofa in the group. Before Gemma can launch into her usual outpouring of fun conversation though Elissa pins me with a serious stare.

"Okay Holly, time to spill the beans, what exactly is going on with Andrew?"

Gemma looks as though her flow of words has just been stopped and she almost splutters. If it wasn't for the seriousness of Elissa's question I would have been in hysterics laughing at the look on Gemma's face.

"I don't know what you mean, there's nothing going on with Andrew. We scened once when I first came to the club, way before I met Bill."

"Nope, not buying it Holly. I saw your face in the car park when he asked you about work, now what is going on?" I've never seen Elissa be so forceful, if I didn't know better I would have said it was Gemma asking the question.

"What's all this about?" Gemma asks.

"That's just what I want to know. He was in the car park when we all arrived. Holly looked scared when he got out of his car, and when he asked her about work she went as white as a sheet." Elissa explains.

How had she seen so much? I thought I had hidden my reactions well.

"Well, now I want to know what's going on too." Gemma adds her piercing stare to Elissa's.

"Has he been hassling you again to play, like he did before."

Suddenly I need to tell someone, if I tell Gemma and Elissa then I'm not dealing with it alone. What if they tell their Sir's though? They would certainly tell Bill all about it.

"You have to promise not to tell anyone, not even Leo and Adam." I say earnestly.

They look at each other with worried faces.

"Honey, we tell them everything, that's the way it works isn't it?" Gemma looks at me seriously.

"Then I'm sorry, but I can't tell you." I say, my voice thick with tears.

"Yes, you can tell us. How about we promise not to tell them anything unless they actually ask us about it? That way we aren't actually keeping secrets. Let's face it they aren't likely to ask are they." I'm surprised to hear this plan come from Elissa, it's normally Gemma who bends the rules.

I think about it for a minute, but I agree with Elissa, they are unlikely to ask, after all no one knows what is going on.

"Okay then, well he's been pressuring me to scene with him. That's what he was doing when you saw him grab my arm, only it's getting so much worse." The first tear rolls down my cheek and I brush it away furiously.

"In what way is it getting worse?" Gemma says at the same time she hands me a tissue.

"He's threatened to tell Bill all sorts of lies about me if I don't play with him, he says Bill will believe him over me, because of all the stuff with Amy."

"You need to tell Bill honey, he will be furious."

"I can't tell him, he's known Andrew for years, he hardly knows me, who do you think he would believe? Besides it got so much worse this week."

"How can it get any worse Holly, he's basically blackmailing you." Elissa sounds shocked.

"He came to my work on Monday, he spoke to my boss, he told him all about me coming here, and what I do here."

Gemma's face sets in fury.

"The bastard, oh my God Holly, you have to tell Bill."

"No, I can't, I don't want to cause any bother, I've caused enough already. He will get bored eventually, and then he will leave me alone."

"Holly if you tell Bill now he will protect you, but if he finds out from someone else he's going to be so mad that you didn't tell him."

"Andrew will move on soon and this thing with Bill probably won't last that long anyway, so the problem will be gone."

"What are you talking about? I've never seen Bill look at anyone the way he looks at you, not even Hannah."

"He must have loved her though, I mean they were together a long time, weren't they?"

"They were, for quite a few years. She really did a number on him. He thought they were heading for a wedding and she was cheating on him for about six months. I don't know how much longer it would have gone on if he hadn't caught them."

"He must have been so hurt." Poor Bill. He was such a lovely man.

"He was, he hasn't been with anyone seriously since, until you." Gemma leans over and hugs me.

"Really?"

"Yes, really. Trust me he is in this for the long term. Which means you should tell him what's going on."

"I really can't, Andrew could tell Bill anything and he would believe him. Especially after what Hannah did to him."

"Sweetie, we won't say anything, but you should really think hard about telling Bill yourself. You need help to deal with this, Andrew needs to be stopped, he might do this to someone else." Elissa takes my hand and gives it a reassuring squeeze.

"You three look very serious, you are normally in fits of giggles by now." Leo threads his fingers in Gemma's hair and turns her head towards him.

"Well we are talking about Doms so it is serious." Gemma winks at him.

"If you carry on being cheeky sweetheart it's going to get very serious for your arse." He has that evil gleam in his eye that says her arse was always in danger tonight, no matter what she did.

Leo takes her hand and leads her over to the play space closest to our seats. He looks deep into her eye's and kisses her gently, then orders her to strip. The contrast to the loving couple and the Dom/sub is right there before my eyes. They have found a way to live the lifestyle within their loving marriage and it's beautiful.

"They are so beautiful together aren't they?" Elissa leans over and whispers to me.

"I know" I sigh. "You have that too though, with Adam." I smile at her.

"We do, he is wonderful." Elissa is practically glowing with happiness.

I am filled with longing for the same thing Gemma and Elissa have found. They have the man they love, who loves them too and the lifestyle to go with it.

"You'll find it too, Gemma is right, the way Bill is with you is so loving, I know he isn't serious most of the time, he does love a joke, but with you he is different. Are you falling in love with him?"

Her question hits me like a truck. Am I? The thought is both exciting and scary, what if he doesn't feel the same? What if he does?

Elissa's laughter pulls me out of my thoughts to look at her smiling face.

"I would say the answer to my question is yes, you have the look of a woman who just realised she loves her man." She leans over and hugs me tight.

# BILL

I walk into the club room and immediately look over to the seating area where Adam and Leo usually sit. There is my little masochist, sitting on her own while Leo is holding a sub spaced Gemma and Adam is just strapping Elissa to the spanking bench.

I walk over and thread my fingers in her hair.

"All on your own girly?" I whisper in her ear.

A shiver runs over her as my breath tickles her neck.

"I'm enjoying watching my friends have fun Sir." She turns and smiles up at me.

"Then, lets watch together." I sit on the sofa and gesture for her to sit on the floor at my feet.

She slips gracefully to the floor and once she is settled I pull her closer so her head can rest against my thigh. She sighs and relaxes into me; a sense of calm seems to envelope us both as we sit and watch Adam and Elissa.

As Adam runs his hand down Elissa's back, I run my hand over Holly's hair. As Adam cups Elissa's bottom, I cup Holly's shoulder. I match them caress for caress, casting an erotic spell around us as we watch their scene unfold.

Adam pulls a flogger from his bag and trails the falls over Elissa's back and legs, I can see her shiver, but I'm not sure if it's because the falls are tickling or with anticipation of what is to come. Of course, it could be both.

I hear Holly sigh as she watches Adam start to flog Elissa, he builds up a rhythm, moving up and down her body. Elissa melts into the leather of the bench, content to lie there and receive what Adam is giving her.

I love to watch the flow of a good scene, one where the Dom and sub seem deeply connected to each other, to the exclusion of everyone else around. Adam swaps to a heavy flogger, and Elissa begins to flinch every time it lands on her skin. Adam is pushing her further than I've seen him do before. She isn't a lover of lots of pain, not like my little masochist.

Holly seems mesmerised by the scene in front of us, she sighs with longing each time the flogger cracks. She will definitely be ready for our scene after watching this.

Just as I think Elissa is going over into sub space, Adam stops the flogging and moves to crouch down at Elissa's head. What is he doing? Why would he interrupt the scene now?

He waits for Elissa to lift her head and look at him, she smiles at him and her face is filled with love.

Adam cups her check gently, then kisses her so tenderly that Holly sighs just watching them together.

"My little mouse, my beautiful Elissa, you have filled my life with love and happiness, you are the other half of me, my heart and my soul. Will you marry me?" He reaches into his pocket and pulls out a glittering diamond ring.

Tears are running down Elissa's face, but she is wearing the biggest smile I've ever seen. I look down at Holly and she also has tears on her cheeks, looking over at Gemma I see a matching set of tear tracks on her face.

"Yes Sir, I would love to marry you." Elissa whispers through her tears.

Adam slips the ring on her finger and kisses her with such passion even I can feel the prick of a tear.

"Okay little mouse, time to really play." Adam says as he stands and moves back to his toy bag.

Their scene begins again and this time Adam takes Elissa right to the edge of sub space and keeps her there for as long as he can. When Elissa is gasping and straining for sub space he gives her an extra hard hit with the paddle and she goes over screaming.

Adam wraps her in a soft blanket and lifts her from the bench into his arms. He cradles her as though she is the most precious person in the world, and to him she must be. Holly leans closer to me as though she is seeking comfort, I pull her up to sit in my lap and hold her tight.

## HOLLY

I don't think I've ever seen anything more beautiful. The love they share is shining out for the whole club to see. Every person who can see them is smiling, more than one woman is dabbing at damp eyes.

My heart feels heavy with the thought that if Amy had done what she set out to do, this moment would never have happened. I'm so incredibly sad to have ever been a part of her nasty plan. I watch as Adam kisses her gently and she relaxes into his arms with total trust. Their love was strong enough to weather the storm though and they hadn't let Amy come between them.

"Are you okay Holly?" Bill whispers against my hair.

"That was so beautiful." I sniff

"It was, Adam caught us all by surprise, although I had a feeling it wouldn't be too much longer."

"I'm so glad Amy didn't manage to spoil everything."

"Me too girly, me too." He pulls me tighter into his arms.

"They belong together."

"Some people just do. Now, I think its time to play, don't you?" He says pushing me to my feet.

Taking my wrist, he leads me through the room to an empty St Andrews cross.

"Clothes off girly."

I rush to obey and I'm stood naked before him before he has taken the leather cuffs out of his bag. He holds out his hand for mine and I feel the depth of my submission to him when I place my much smaller hand into his. Just that small gesture is enough, he could just take my hand if he wanted to, but he waits for me to give it to him, just as he waits for me to give him my submission and my trust.

"Thank you girly." He murmurs and he buckles the leather around my wrist, checking with his fingers that it isn't too tight.

He holds his hand out for my other wrist and attaches the cuff to that one too, then come the ankle cuffs. There is something very moving about seeing this big proud man kneeling at my feet to gently strap cuffs to my ankles, it brings tears to my eyes, I want to pull him up off the floor to stand tall.

He looks up from the floor and the desire in his eyes starts a fire deep inside me.

"You are so beautiful." He whispers. "And you are mine."

I want so much to be his, I want him to love me. I think Elissa is right and I am falling head over heels with this funny, caring, Sadist.

I look over to where Adam is still holding Elissa wrapped snuggly in her blanket and I can see the diamond on her finger twinkle in the lights from the dance floor. Fairy tales did come true sometimes then.

I look down at Bill and smile at him, for the moment at least he is my Sir, and I am going to enjoy every moment. Suddenly the need for pain rushes back in and I am wound tighter than a spring, just like I have been most of the week. The fact that I know Bill can and will give me the pain I need drives my need higher.

He pulls me forward and clips the cuffs to the four corners of the cross, then he steps back, I feel chilled without his heat at my back, and a shiver runs through me. I turn my head to the side to get a little more comfortable and see Andrew stood to one side a nasty leer on his face.

I stiffen and turn my head to face the other way, I didn't want to see his face while Bill was sending me to my good place, I can't let him invade my good space.

"Does something hurt Holly? Are the cuffs too tight?" Damn Bill for seeing my every reaction.

"No Sir." My voice is barely above a whisper.

"You stiffened as though something hurt. What is it?"

"Sir, could I please have a blindfold? I want to get inside my own head and I can't if I can see all these people." It was partially true, it was just one person in particular I don't want inside my head with the pain. The pain is mine.

"Well since you asked so nicely and your reasons are good, yes you can girly." He reaches into his bad and pulls out a padded black blindfold with an elastic strap.

"Thank you, Sir."

He slips the soft fabric over my eyes and the world becomes black, I instantly feel calmer. I know Andrew is probably still watching, but at least now I don't have to see him.

"Are you okay with the noise Holly? Or do you need ear defenders too?" He asks.

Do I? The quiet would be different, it would put me in my own silent dark space where I can drift and feel without thinking.

"That would be really good, thank you Sir."

I can hear him rummaging in his bag and then I feel the hard ear defenders come to rest on my head, and the world is silent and dark.

The first sting of pain flares on my arse cheek and the shock of it sends me up on my tip toes. The rush of feeling that spreads over my whole body sends my spirit soring, this is what I have been needing all week. The need to escape from the real world, especially the ugliness that is my situation with Andrew.

I don't want to think about him now, I won't have this part of my life tainted by thoughts of him, these feelings belong to me and Bill, no one else.

I feel the sharp sting of pain as Bill uses what I think is a whip, he moves all over my back and bum, there is no pattern at all and I can't focus on the hits, just the sensation of the sharp sting. I squirm in frustration, needing a steady rhythm to really relax.

I feel the gentle warmth of Bills hand as he checks my skin, but I don't want gentle. I make a moan of protest which he must have been able to hear. He pinches the skin of my bottom sharply in warning then continues to use the whip.

Soon each sweep of sensation overlaps the last and I can feel my grip on reality begin to slip. With my eyes closed behind the blindfold and no sound to guide me I lose my sense of where I am stood. My brain gives up trying to process information and just concentrates on the only thing it can, the sting of pain.

I feel the knot of tension inside me unravel and my muscles unclench as I slip further into the space inside my own head. No one intrudes on my special cloud of feeling, not even my own thoughts. I am floating away on a cloud of stinging pain until I find the heaven of total sub space.

## BILL

It is such a joy to watch her relax more as our scene develops. She had seemed so tense when she arrived and so emotional when I had come to find her talking to Elissa, something had been bothering her. Maybe it was the same thing that had bothered me, I had really missed her this week.

I flick the dressage whip over and over again, catching her skin with just the very tip, each flick delivers a small concentrated sting and I can see it is beginning to overwhelm her senses. Her shoulders have dropped down and she is leaning more heavily against the cross.

Time to switch to the cane I think, I select a thick solid one from my bag, it will deliver a good thud followed by a sting. She flinches in surprise at the new sensation, but then she moans with appreciation. I push her further and she responds by melting into the sensation, she is relaxing before my eyes, and my own muscles relax in response.

I can feel myself getting into a good zone, one where I know instinctively just where to land the next blow of the cane, how quickly to deliver the next one, when to pause, when to rush in. I've hit Dom space and it feels amazing, we are so in tune with each other, although at the moment all she is aware of is the pain.

The world is lost to her and she is free to be what ever she likes inside her own little cloud of peace. She is beautiful in her surrender, brave and beautiful, and mine.

The stripes of red from the cane are decorating her arse with neat straight lines, when I run my hand over the marks, her skin is hot to my touch. She hisses as my nails scrape over the stripes and I laugh softly. I push her further and soon she is so deep into sub space she isn't reacting to the cane at all. Time to stop and hold her while she floats.

Holding a blanket over her back I pull her away from the cross a little to lean against me while I unclip the cuffs from the rings on the cross. She sags against me and I lower her gently to the floor while I unclip the ankle cuffs and clear away my toys and clean down the play space ready for the next people to scene.

She is sitting huddled inside the blanket, still with the ear defenders on and the blindfold in place. Remembering the last time we scened in the club I decide to leave the ear defenders on for a while. The noise of the club had made her anxious when she was in sub space last time.

Looking around to find somewhere to sit I notice Andrew watching us closely. He notices my gaze and smiles at me.

"Good scene Bill, she spaces really well doesn't she?"

I don't like the way he is looking at Holly, she is mine and he shouldn't have that possessive look in his eye, I know they have scened in the past, but that didn't give him the right to look at her like that.

"If you'll excuse me I need to see to Holly." I turn my back on him and pick Holly up from the floor.

When I turn back he is gone. I walk over to the seating area and sit, settling Holly snugly on my lap. She moans softly and relaxes against my chest. I pull the blindfold off, but leave the ear defenders on. She needs to come back to herself in her own time, not because the noise of the room yanks her back.

Relaxing back into the sofa I let the warm satisfying feeling of holding Holly close fill me. It's been so long since I've felt this deep a sense of satisfaction. Looking down into her relaxed face I'm overwhelmed by how deep my feelings for her are. How have I fallen for her so quickly?

I love her ability to tease just as much as her love of pain, but I love her vulnerability too. She needs to be loved and cared for, she deserves someone who will treat her like she's precious, but will also give her what she needs and craves. That someone is definitely me. I just hope she agrees.

Her eyes drift open, but I can see she's not really back from sub space. She looks up at me with total trust in her eyes and her sigh is one of contentment. A small smile curves her lips as her eyes drift closed again. She's not ready to come back yet.

# HOLLY

I am floating in a warm silent space; my head is resting against something hard and warm and I can feel tight bands around my back and ribs. The tight feeling is comforting, as though it is grounding me and stopping me from floating away and getting lost in my own head.

I feel safe, protected and calm. Like I've been washed clean, all the stress and anxiety from earlier has floated away. As my brain switches back on I realise that it's Bills arms I can feel holding me tight. He gave me what I needed to free myself from the stress and then kept me safe while I floated in my own head.

I try to open my eyes, but they feel too heavy, I finally manage to lift my eye lids and look up to see Bills eyes staring down at me. There is so much emotion in his gaze it scares me a little and I shut my eyes again to hide from it.

Could he be feeling the same about me as I was about him? Could I dare to hope we might have a future together? Elissa is right, I do love him, the thought makes me tremble. I want to hide in sub space again, but now my mind has switched back on I can't.

I wriggle and gasp as my sore behind rubs against the blanket. Opening my eyes again I see his laughing face looking down at me. His lips move, but I can't hear anything, panic fills me, why can't I hear anything.

His smile fades and he reaches over to pull something from my head. Oh! Ear defenders, that explains why I can't hear anything. The noise of the club rushes in and fills my head.

"I said was that a little uncomfortable girly?" His smile is back.

"Just a little, Sir." I squirm again just to feel the discomfort.

"Have some water Holly." He holds out a bottle of cool water and I gulp it down.

Why am I so thirsty? I must have been gasping and panting a lot during our scene. Suddenly I remember that Andrew had been stood watching us and I look around in panic to see if he's still there, but apart from a couple of people walking past we are alone.

I let out a relieved breath and relax against Bill again.

"You definitely needed that girly; do you want to tell me what had you so uptight and anxious?"

"It's just been a long week, work has been busy and quite stressful." Well the visit from Andrew had made it stressful.

"Has work calmed down now, or is it still stressful?"

"It's better now, I had a good chat with my boss and I feel much happier." That at least was the truth, Jackson had been lovely.

"You know you can tell me anything Holly, I will protect you from the world." He lifts my chin to look into my eyes.

The words are on the tip of my tongue ready to pour out, but I still don't think he would believe me over Andrew.

"No one can protect someone from everything, that's not how life works, it doesn't even happen in fairy tales." I say sadly.

"I will protect you Holly, you can count on that." His grip on my chin tightens.

"Do you promise?" Maybe everything would be okay, maybe he would believe me.

"Holly, I will always protect you, never doubt that."

I bury my face in the hollow of his shoulder and breathe in his unique scent, I feel safe in his arms, if only I could stay here forever.

"Now are you feeling up to going to congratulate the happy couple, or do you need a little longer?"

"Oh, I would love to."

"Off you go to get dressed then, I will wait for you here." I jump up off his knee and rush to the changing room to get dressed.

Elissa must be so happy, she loves Adam so much and he obviously loves her just as much. She is such a lovely lady, she deserves all the happiness in the world. I am so glad Amy didn't get her way, so glad that Adam convinced Elissa his feelings were true.

Are Bills feelings just as true? I have fallen in love with him, and I want this to last, I'm already deeper in than I ever intended to be. If it ended now it would hurt so much, but if it ends further down the line it will be devastating.

Putting aside my pessimistic thoughts I rush to get dressed before Bill comes looking for me.

# BILL

She comes rushing out of the changing room door as though she is escaping a fire. When she reaches me she immediately kneels at my feet.

"I'm sorry I took so long Sir." She gushes her apology.

"You weren't that long Holly, and I didn't give you a time limit." Her look of relief makes me laugh.

"It felt like I'd been ages."

"Stop worrying so much Holly. Let's go and see Adam and Elissa." I pull her up from the floor and wrap my arm around her waist, pulling her in close to my side as we walk around the dance floor to where our friends are sitting.

Elissa is positively glowing, she is kneeling at Adams feet with her head resting against his thigh, a beautiful smile on her face as she looks at her twinkling engagement ring.

"Adam, congratulations, I'm so pleased for you both." I shake his hand and sit down, pulling Holly down to the floor beside me.

She looks up at me for permission to speak to Elissa.

"Good girl Holly, Adam, permission for my sub to speak to your sub?"

"Of course, in fact why don't the girls sit together and chat, I'm sure they are bursting at the seams to talk weddings." He gestures to Gemma and Holly and points to the sofa in the next seating area.

The girls jump up and are soon sat in deep discussion and admiring Elissa's ring.

"That's it, we've lost them for the rest of the night now." I say with a laugh.

"It looks like it." Leo agrees.

"Let them plan, at least they enjoy the planning, not like me." Adam laughs.

"Holly looks more relaxed now, you must have had a good scene, she looked so tense and anxious when she arrived. Do you know what was wrong?" Leo asks.

"No, she says work has been stressful, but I get the feeling there's more to it than that. She's not sharing though."

"Well if she won't tell you there isn't much you can do to help." Adam sympathises.

"Maybe it is just work stuff, and I can't really help with that apart from giving support to deal with it, which I can do without knowing exactly what the issue is." I should let it go and trust her, if there was a real problem surely, she would tell me.

"You have to start trusting people Bill, not everyone is like Hannah." As usual Leo is the voice of reason.

"I know, I don't think I realised until now just how much she messed me up." I had avoided relationships since Hannah.

"You've looked happier and more yourself since Holly came back into the club." Adam chips in.

"I've been happy."

"You've been happy on the surface, you've laughed and joked, but you haven't been truly happy for years. It's good to see the Sadist in you get to come out and play again too."

"I have really enjoyed my scenes with Holly, it's like my body is saying finally!"

"When you find the person that fits with you and your kinks, it is a special thing. It's hard enough finding the right person for you romantically, when you try to find someone who fits your kinks too it becomes almost impossible." Leo had been really lucky, he had found Gemma really early on in his journey.

"Yet here we all sit, having done just that." Says Adam.

Have I done that? Is Holly my forever woman? It definitely feels like she is, I feel like myself around her. I can share all the parts of myself with her, rather than just the fun joking me. She allows me to be myself just as I free her to be herself. I love who I am with her, and I love her.

The realisation hits me square in the chest. I am in love with Holly.

"Only just realised, have you?" Leo laughs.

"Realised what?"

"That you love her of course."

"Do you never get tired of being right all the time?" I say good heartedly.

"No, I quite like it really." He looks so smug.

"So, when will the wedding be Adam?" I feel the need to deflect attention from myself.

"I haven't thought about that yet, I needed to make sure she said yes first."

"I don't think there was ever any doubt about her answer."

"Well, you never know, but anyway I don't think I'm going to have a lot of say in the wedding plans, not if Gemma is involved."

"My wife is nothing if not dedicated, just watch your bank balance when they go wedding shopping." Leo laughs.

Gemma is a very determined shopper and it was her favourite pass time with Elissa, and now it seemed Holly too.

"How's Henry doing? I haven't seen him for a couple of weeks." Adam asks.

"He's feeling better, it's no fun getting chicken pox at his age, he caught it from his Nephew. He rang today to say the last of the spots have almost cleared, he should be back in next week."

"I bet he's going stir crazy being stuck at home all the time, he's always so busy." Leo knew just as I did how busy Henry was at work, and then he came to cover my nights off here. His job was so busy and stressful that I think the club is how he unwinds.

"I wouldn't like to be doing his day job, that's for sure." Adam agrees.

"No, me neither. I can't imagine some of the hard decisions he has to make every day, I don't know how he does it."

Henry is a bed manager at the local hospital, we all know about the bed crisis in hospitals, and with winter approaching it would only get worse. Henry always switched off in the club though, it was his down time. It was just a shame he didn't have a sub at the moment.

# HOLLY

"Your ring is beautiful Elissa, you look so happy." She looks all lit up inside, happiness is practically shining out from her.

"I am, I was so surprised, I had no idea he was going to propose, let alone tonight."

"I didn't think it would be much longer." Gemma says.

"Did you know?" Elissa asks.

"No, I swear I didn't know when, I just thought it wouldn't be long off. He loves you so much, of course he was going to propose." She smiles.

"I'm so lucky."

"So is Adam, he's just as lucky to have you as you are to have him." Gemma says firmly.

"Well it seems he agrees with you for some reason." The smile fills her face and her eyes are sparkling with tears.

"We need to get planning the wedding." I can hear the excitement in Gemma's voice.

"Hang on, I've only been engaged for five minutes." Elissa laughs.

"Weddings take a lot of organising." Gemma says defensively.

"I know they do, but it's only going to be a small wedding. There aren't that many people to invite."

"What about your family?" I ask.

"There is only my Sister and I only got back in touch with her recently. She might not want to come." Oh no, I didn't mean to upset her, I need to bring back the happiness to her face.

"Of course she will want to come, she's your Sister. Is she older or younger than you?"

"Sophie is younger than me, she's twenty-two."

"And she will be there, hopefully in a bridesmaid dress." Gemma says firmly.

"What sort of dress do you want?" Every woman has imagined her wedding dress.

"Something romantic and lacy." There it is, the sparkle of excitement is back.

We spend quite a long time talking about weddings and everything to do with them, until our men decide we've had long enough for girly talk. Adam pulls Elissa onto the dance floor and holds her close, they aren't really dancing, just swaying, lost in their own little world.

I sigh and then laugh when I hear Gemma do the same.

"Typical, they have gone all mushy now." Bill laughs.

"I know, it is romantic though." Leo is watching Adam and Elissa.

"Don't you start, it's bad enough the girls getting all mushy." Bill pokes him in the ribs.

The rest of the night is spent in fun conversation and lots of laughter as we all catch the good mood from Adam and Elissa. All thoughts of Andrew are pushed to the back of my mind for the night.

I spend the weekend with Bill at his flat, we cook together, relax over breakfast reading the paper, and snuggle on the sofa watching movies. I am so relaxed and I really recharge my batteries.

When I walk through the doors at work on Monday morning I have a big happy smile on my face.

"Someone looks like they had a good weekend." Jackson says as he comes out of his office.

"I did thank you, did you have a good one?"

"Very chilled out thank you. So, the romance is still going well then?"

"It is, really well." It feels like my smile has taken over my whole face.

"Wow! You are positively glowing Holly, congratulations."

"I think I'm in love."

"It looks like it. How is the other situation? Have you had any more trouble from him?"

"Not since he goaded me outside the club on Friday night no. He was expecting me to have got fired after he came in here and I think he was quite angry when that didn't happen." I shiver as I remember just how angry he had been.

"Be careful Holly, I don't think he's the type to give up easily."

"He'll get bored soon." Even in my own ears I don't sound convinced.

"Have you told Bill yet?" He asks reproachfully.

"No, if it goes away I won't have to tell him, I don't want to cause any more trouble in the club."

"I don't think it works that way sweetie. From my limited knowledge of your lifestyle, he's going to be really pissed when he finds out."

"Well hopefully he never will."

Jacksons words echo in my head as I sit at my desk and begin work. I just want the situation to go away. It feels so unfair that when I finally fall in love, it's overshadowed by Andrew and his threats. I try and concentrate on my work, and soon it's lunch time. I head out to find something inspiring for lunch and bump into Gemma and Elissa just outside my building.

"Hi girls, what are you doing here?"

"We came to take you for lunch." Says Elissa.

"What's the occasion?" I ask in surprise.

"No occasion, just because." I think Gemma is trying for an innocent tone, but I'm not fooled.

"Yeah right, and I am the Queen of Sheba." I laugh.

"You are so busted." Elissa splutters.

"Okay, you've got me, I do have a favour to ask you." Gemma looks sheepish.

"Let's go get lunch before you tell her."

I follow them to a deli just over the road from work and we order lunch and find a table.

"So, what favour did you need to ask me?"

"I need some help, with planning the engagement party." I can't imagine Gemma needing much help to plan anything to be honest.

"What help do you need?" I've never hosted a party so I have no idea what planning one would involve.

"With ideas mainly, Elissa has decided she wants to hold the party in her garden, which means we will have to keep our fingers crossed for good weather. It doesn't matter too much if it's cold, but if it rains we will be in big trouble." Gemma rolls her eyes in Elissa's direction.

"It has to be in the garden, and on the beach, so much happened in the garden and on the beach." A blush spreads over Elissa's cheeks and I can just imagine what sort of things happened in the garden.

"Well it will just have to stay dry for you then, but just in case why don't you get a big gazebo and put it up on the beach, that way if it does happen to rain a bit people can stay dry." I suggest.

"Great idea, see I knew I was right to ask for your help." Gemma exclaims.

"Won't it get cold once the sun goes down though?"

"I've already thought of that, fire pits!" She says as though she invented them.

"Okay, so when is this engagement party? How long do we have to plan?" I have an awful feeling it's probably not long.

"Oh, we have ages." Gemma says with a casual wave of her hand.

"Gemma, that's a lie." Elissa gasps.

"How long Gemma?" I ask.

"Weeks." She says vaguely.

"How many weeks exactly?" I demand.

"God, details details. Why is everyone so caught up on the date? If we all spent more time planning and less time worrying about how long we have, it would be planned already."

"How many weeks Gemma?" I pin her with a stare.

"Five, now can we get on with the planning?"

Well, it could be worse, not much worse, but knowing Gemma it could have been three days.

"Do I need to ask who decided on the date?" I look at Elissa.

"You could, but you probably know the answer without asking." She jerks her head in Gemma's direction.

"We can't leave it too long, not if Elissa wants it in the garden, everyone would freeze if we wait much longer, it is almost winter you know." She says defensively.

I suppose she does have a point. Gemma pulls out a notepad and a pen and starts assigning tasks to us all. There is so much to do, and it looks like all three of us are going to be really busy between now and the party. We devise a plan of action as we eat our sandwiches, and we got so engrossed in our planning I was almost late back to work.

# BILL

I'm sorting through the membership cards, pulling out lapsed members and writing out new cards for the ones that are full when the front door of the club opens and Henry walks in.

"Henry, it's good to see you, how are you feeling now?"

"Loads better, I always wondered why my Mum kept making me play with all those spotty children when I was a child, now I know. Chicken pox is so much worse for an adult. I don't know what was worse, the itching from the spots, or the itching from the growing beard, because I couldn't shave."

"I hope you resisted scratching." I laugh.

"I did mostly, I decided that I would choose one spot to scratch whenever the urge became too much, of course I chose one that no one would see."

"That's not a bad plan, and it seems to have worked, you don't have any on your face or arms." He looked really well.

"I'm full of good ideas like that, and I only have a couple of the more serious spots left."

"So, are you ready to come back?"

"Oh my god yes! I'm losing my mind being stuck at home. I will be back to the day job next week, but if I could get back to my shifts in here it would help."

"That would be brilliant, if you are sure you are up to it, I could use a night off."

"Have I missed much while I've been away?"

"Adam proposed to Elissa in the middle of a scene."

"Oh fantastic, good for him, mind you I don't think any of us are that surprised. How are things with you and Holly? Is she still coming in?"

"Yes, things are great, progressing well."

"Are you actually getting serious about her?" He looks surprised.

"I am, it's serious, I'm in this for the long term."

"Good for you, and does she feel the same?"

Well that is the million-dollar question, does she? We haven't talked about long term, I haven't told her I love her, suddenly that feels like a big mistake. I should have told her the minute I realised.

"I don't know, we haven't spoken about it."

"Well, don't you think it's time you did?"

"I think it just might be."

Henry was a good man, a wise one too considering he was only twenty-five, that was probably a lot to do with his job, you can't take on that amount of responsibility without growing up in a hurry.

"Just do it Bill, life is too short to put things off, I see it every day at work, people who think they have so much time, and suddenly their time is up."

He looks so serious, how many times had he seen this happen? I couldn't do his job, not the way he does, and I definitely couldn't do his job and stay sane. It must be so hard not to bring the work home with him, but somehow, he seems to manage, today is one of the few times I've heard him talk about work in a serious way.

"Just do it Bill, don't wait."

I know he's right, I should tell her how I feel, there isn't a reason not to and so many reasons for me to tell her.

We carry on chatting about happenings at the club and Henry loses his serious air as the afternoon passes. He really had missed the club. We plan our shifts and Henry takes a couple more shifts to give me a couple of extra nights off.

"So, is there anyone new coming in I should know about?" It's an innocent enough question, but I sense the real question behind it, Henry has been looking for the right sub for far too long.

So far though he hasn't found the right fit with anyone.

"No one lately no." I really wish I had a different answer for him.

"Maybe one day the right person will walk through that door." His tone isn't very hopeful.

# HOLLY

The next week passes in a flurry of activity, with work and then all the planning for the party I hardly have a free minute. It's a relief when it finally gets to Friday night and work is done. I'm meeting Bill for dinner before the club opens.

Thanks to Henry being back, we have at least been able to get together a couple of nights during the week. I definitely don't feel as anxious and in need of a scene as I did last week, work has been good and nothing else has happened with Andrew. I'm hoping he has given up and will leave me alone from now on.

I take my time getting ready, I want to feel special tonight, I want to be my best for Bill. I pull a deep blue dress from my wardrobe and head to the shower. I shampoo my hair twice, luxuriating in the heat of the water and the feeling of washing away my long week. Leaving a conditioning mask to work its magic, I shave my legs and use my expensive shower oil.

Once I'm done in the shower I blow dry my hair, it gleams with a healthy shine in the bedroom lights. I put on my bra and thong, and slip the silky dress over my head. My dress swirls around me when I twirl in front of the full-length mirror. I look at myself from head to toe and I am filled with confidence, I look good, and more importantly, I look happy.

I am happy, despite all the stress from the Andrew situation, I have never been happier. I finally feel like I have found my true self, and it feels so good. To be so comfortable with who I am like I never have before is a gift I never expected. Loving Bill is something I never could have dreamed of.

Even if he never loves me back, it will still be a special time to remember.

I get into my car with a bubble of excitement fizzing away inside, it was a night of endless possibilities. Bill is already there waiting for me when I get to the restaurant, he stands as I walk over to the table.

"Holly, you look stunning, you take my breath away."

He looks really good, he's wearing black dress pants and a black shirt with the sleeves rolled up to his elbows. The open collar of the shirt reveals the strong column of his neck and a curl of dark chest hair.

"You look very sexy tonight Sir." I say with a shy smile.

"Well thank you Holly, but we aren't in the club now, it's Bill." He holds the chair out for me and pushes it in once I am seated.

"Thank you, Bill."

"Have you had a good day? You look happy." He takes my hand in his and his thumb strokes the sensitive skin on the inside of my wrist.

"I am happy, life is good."

"I hope I'm one of the reasons life is making you so happy."

"You are indeed, one of the big reasons." I blush.

"Tell me the other reasons." He demands, we may not be in the club, but he is still a Dom through and through.

"There are lots of reasons, I have friends now, Elissa and Gemma have welcomed me into their friendship and it feels good. Work is going well, I have a better working relationship with my boss." I can feel my smile stretching across my face.

The waiter comes over to take our drinks order and give us the menu, we're both quiet while we are deciding what to order. Once the waiter has brought our drinks and taken our food order, we are left alone again.

"So, tell me, what else is good today?" He takes a sip of his drink and looks intently at me.

"I am, I'm me, finally and me is good." I can feel the warm glow deep inside begin to swell and grow.

"It sounds like the first time you've realised that."

"That's because it is, I've found myself, the real me and you helped me set her free."

"Sometimes we all need a little help to open the door and step through."

"I doubt you've ever needed that sort of help." I laugh softly.

"Now that's where you would be wrong girly."

"Really?" Now I'm curious.

"Really, only yesterday actually. Someone pointed out to me that I was putting something off because I was being a coward." His gaze is fixed intently on me.

"You being a coward? Never, I can't imagine you being scared of anything."

"Everyone has something they are scared of Holly, and I would say most people are scared of being hurt emotionally." He looks sad.

"Hannah really hurt you, didn't she?" I take hold of his hand in sympathy.

"She did, yes, but what I didn't realise until yesterday was that I have been holding part of myself separate from the world since then. I didn't let anyone in just in case I got hurt again."

He was letting me see his vulnerabilities, he was trusting me not to hurt him with the knowledge that could hurt him most. He was showing me that even though he is my Sir he is also human, with human frailties and issues.

"And who opened the door for you?" Who had been brave enough to point it out to him?

"It was Henry. He pointed out that life is too short to wait, we should take every chance at happiness we can find."

"How did someone so young get to be so wise?"

"It's his job I think, he sees a lot of people who did leave it too late. He is a sensitive soul too though, he feels everything too deeply."

"Why is he still single? He should have someone to love."

"He hasn't found the right person yet, unlike me. I have found exactly the right person to love."

I gasp in shock; did he just say he loves me?

"You have?"

BILL

"I have, I love you Holly. You say I helped you find your true self, well you brought me back to my true self. You have given me back what Hannah stole from me."

She is staring at me as though I've grown an extra head, is she just shocked, or totally horrified?

"Wow Henry is good." She laughs. "All that from just one conversation."

"It was all there, it just needed me to be brave enough to say it." I shrug.

"Then if you have been brave, so can I, I love you too." She takes a big breath as though that did indeed take a lot of bravery.

Then suddenly she smiles at me. I let out the breath I hadn't realised I'd been holding and smile back at her. We are both sitting there smiling at each other like fools when the waiter brings our food.

"I wasn't sure how you felt, I haven't been sure of how you viewed our relationship, if it was a short-term thing to you, I've sometimes had the feeling you are holding something back from me." It was still a niggle at the back of my mind.

"I was hoping it wold turn into something lasting, but I thought you would lose interest and move on."

"Is that why you were holding part of yourself back? Because you thought we wouldn't last?" So, it was a self-preservation thing.

"Partly yes, but also because I am so used to dealing with things on my own, I've been on my own for such a long time."

"Have you been in a relationship long term before?" I'm curious, she has never mentioned anyone serious.

"No, I dated a couple of men, but you couldn't really call it a relationship, let alone a long term one." She laughs.

"So, you've never lived with anyone?"

"No, I've lived alone since my parents died, I like the independence, but it does get lonely sometimes." I'm sure it does, I can't even imagine being alone for so many years, I had thought my few years alone since Hannah was a long time.

"Well you aren't alone any more, you can count on me when you need someone, I'll always be here." A shadow of something crosses her face, and I can't help wondering if something is still lurking.

"And you really love me?" She looks uncertain.

I reach over the table to cup her cheek, and she leans into my caress.

"Yes Holly, I love you." Her smile is dazzling. "Stay with me tonight."

"Yes please." Her laugh is joyous.

As we leave the restaurant after dinner she grabs hold of my hand and leans against my shoulder. It does feel as though we have truly opened the doors to our relationship. It's a shame I have to man the front desk tonight, it would have been good to seal our relationship with a scene. That will have to wait until tomorrow night, of course that doesn't mean we can't celebrate in another way once the door to my flat closes later.

The queue to come in to the club keeps us busy for the first couple of hours, but once it goes a little quieter we are able to talk some more. Mostly we talk about trivia, what we love to eat, favourite films and holiday destinations. Holly gets really animated when she warms to a subject, and I'm amused when it is the topic of food that gets her passion up.

"I don't care what you say, mushrooms are the food of the devil." She is quite determined.

"So, are there any other foods you wish to condemn to hell?" I can't stop laughing.

"Peas and baked beans." She says without hesitation.

"Any more?"

"No that's about it. How about you?"

"I will eat anything, there isn't much I don't eat."

"Even twiglets?" She winks at me.

"Yes, even twiglets."

"Well, if you think you're kissing me after you've been eating twiglets you can think again."

I grab a handful of her hair and yank her head back; her eyes widen in surprise and her mouth drops open at the sudden plunge into the power exchange. Taking advantage of her parted lips I plunder her mouth in a scorching kiss.

When I pull back her eyes are glazed and she's short of breath.

"Just remember where you are girly, If I want to kiss you after eating twiglets I will, unless you make twiglets a hard limit."

"Yes Sir."

I hear the door open behind me, but I keep my gaze focused on her for long seconds to enforce my point. Once I'm sure she feels the full extent of my control I turn to see that it was Henry who came in. He is standing at a respectful distance waiting for our moment to end and I smile my thanks at him.

"Good evening Henry, are you well."

"I'm very well thank you, is it busy tonight?" He takes a pen to sign in and smiles at Elissa.

"About average really, not too bad. Are you planning to play?"

"That depends who's in tonight, but knowing my luck lately probably not."

"Just a social night for you then?" Lots of people did come into the club just to socialise and catch up with friends.

# HOLLY

As Henry stands up from the desk he winks at me, and with a smile he leans over to whisper in my ear.

"I hate twiglets too, I'd add it to your hard limit list if I were you, or at some point in the not too distant future you will find yourself being kissed by a mouth that tastes like something you scraped off your shoe."

An involuntary giggle escapes me, when I look over and see Bill's scowl it grows into a full out laugh.

"Be careful girly, they aren't on your limit list yet and there are twiglets behind the bar."

That stops my laugh immediately and I busy myself straightening the top of the already tidy desk. I can tell Bill is finding it funny though, but I really don't want to risk twiglet breath. The night passes quietly and closing time is suddenly upon us.

"Go through to the flat Holly, I will do the final checks and lock up."

"Do you want me to do anything while I'm waiting, fix you a drink or a snack maybe?"

"I would like you to relax in a bubble bath, I will come and find you as soon as I'm done out here."

"Yes Sir" He leans in and gives me a gentle kiss, then slaps me hard on the arse before walking away whistling.

I start the hot water running as soon as I enter the flat, there is a bottle of my favourite bubble bath sitting on the shelf waiting for me, so I pour a generous amount under the stream of water. Before long the bathroom is filled with a wonderful steam cloud of fragrance and I'm sinking down into the hot bubbles.

Resting my head back against the roll top of the bath, I can feel all my muscles begin to relax and unwind. The busy week washes away, leaving me calm and relaxed.

I must have drifted off to sleep because the next thing I know I feel rough finger tips brushing across my nipple. The water is much cooler too, how long had I been asleep, it felt like I had only closed my eyes a few seconds ago.

"It's dangerous to fall asleep in the bath girly, you could drown." His fingers continue to brush my nipples in a lazy rhythm.

"I didn't think I was that tired, but the water was hot and I must have relaxed a little too much. How long have I been in here?"

"About thirty minutes." His fingers trail down over my belly, then across to my hip bone, then back to the other hip bone.

"I should get out then, you must be tired." I move to sit up, but his firm hand pushes me back against the side of the bath.

"Stay very still Holly, I like the way your skin feels in the water."

I give in and relax again, I could lie here and let his magical fingers relax me even more.

"Close your eyes and just feel."

I am floating in a world of sensation, the warmth of the water, the scent of the bubbles, the feel of his fingers. Unlike our scenes in the club though this was a gentle, sensual way to find my happy place.

Lips close around my nipple and the gentle suction is pushing me further into arousal. Fingers continue to brush over the other nipple, keeping in time with the suction of his mouth. The tingle of arousal begins to flutter in my pussy and I lift my hips trying to entice him to explore with those maddening finger tips.

"Keep still Holly, or everything stops, we are going at my pace, not yours." He waits until I relax back under the water before he continues with his slow torment.

He teases me with a touch that is just enough to get me aroused, but light enough not to cause any real friction against my sensitive needy body. If he keeps this up I will never orgasm and I am likely to expire with frustration.

His finger finally comes to rest gently against my clit and he moves it slowly against first one side, then the other side. Up one side, a pause of slight pressure right on top, then slowly down the other side.

I need more, or I'll never reach the climax I'm yearning for.

"Stop pushing for it Holly, you need to relax into it and let the feeling develop slowly on it's own. Focus on your breathing, and let whatever happens happen. Trust me." He keeps the same rhythm and speed with his hand as he talks to me.

I breath in slowly, then let the breathe out on a sigh. Soon the only things I am aware of are the sound of my breathing and the feeling of his finger, repeating its circuit over and over again. I lie still and just let it happen, even if I don't climax, this still feels really good.

The sensation drifts along with me into my scented world of darkness, never changing, never rushing or forced, just the constant movement of his finger over my folds.

I sigh in contentment, and I feel my limbs float in the water as they become limp and boneless. I am so relaxed that I don't notice how aroused I've become. Suddenly an orgasm spreads over me, I fall into it so gently it's like laying back onto a soft bed.

There is nothing frantic or strained about it, it just washes over me like soft summer rain, bringing tears to my eyes at the beauty of it.

"Open your eyes Holly." He whispers.

I look up at him and he's smiling softly down at me.

"You look so beautiful, that was moving to watch."

"It was beautiful to feel too." I sigh.

"You are beautiful." His fingers caress my face gently.

# BILL

"You make me feel like the most beautiful woman in the world." She whispers and a tear spills over to run down her cheek.

"Hey, don't cry, there's nothing to cry about." I pull her up into my arms and hold her tight.

"That just felt so beautiful and intense, I can't help it." She sniffs.

"Come on, lets get you dry and into bed." I wrap her in a big soft towel and carry her into the bedroom.

I rub her skin dry and tuck her under the duvet to keep warm.

"I'm just going to get a quick shower, you just relax for a while."

I shower quickly, and get dry in the bathroom, when I walk into the bedroom she is fast asleep. Her hair is spread out across my pillow like spun gold, long eye lashes rest against her pink cheeks, her lips are slightly parted and her soft breaths of sleep come slow and deep.

I have never seen anything more beautiful and precious. I climb into bed and pull her back against me, I'm surrounded by the scent of her hair and her skin is so soft against mine. She wriggles in her sleep, settling the lush cheeks of her arse more snugly against me.

How the hell am I ever going to sleep with her body so temptingly close to mine? I close my eyes and after what feels like a long time I can feel myself finally start to drift off to sleep.

It's still dark when I wake, and for a few seconds I'm not sure what has woken me, but then I feel cool caressing fingers around my rapidly hardening cock.

"What are you up to girly? Don't you know it's dangerous to wake a sleeping Sadist?"

"I didn't think you'd mind too much." She giggles.

"What time is it?" I don't feel like I've been asleep that long.

"I have no idea, but I don't care."

Her fingers tighten, and she begins to slide her hand firmly up and down my cock in a slow steady rhythm. She blows across the tip and a shiver runs over me.

"You little tease." I gasp.

"Who me? Never!" Her sexy laugh only arouses me more.

Her tongue sweeps up the whole length of my cock, then her lips close over the head. She teases me even more by just keeping the tip in her mouth and not moving. She thinks she has me under her control, how wrong she is. If she's going to play with fire she's going to get burned.

My hips surge up off the bed, catching her by surprise and filling her mouth full of my hard cock.

"If you're going to wake me up at an ungodly hour with a blow job, then give me a blow job, don't tease." I growl at her.

She pulls off my cock with a very satisfying slurping noise.

"Yes Sir." She says firmly, and then she takes my whole length into her mouth in one downward plunge of her mouth.

Her tongue flicks against the head of my cock on each downward stroke, her teeth graze every time she pulls up. She's driving me wild and I'm soon groaning with the need to come. She runs her nails up the inside of my thighs and across my balls and I jerk as though I've been electrocuted.

Suddenly she takes me right to the back of her throat and swallows, the feel of her throat squeezing me tight sends me over the edge and my come fills her mouth. She swallows every drop and then licks me clean.

"Thank you, Holly, come up here." She moves up the bed and kisses me gently.

"You're welcome Sir." She whispers and I can hear the smile in her voice.

"You're very good at that."

"I'm glad you think so, maybe I'll have to do it again."

"Be careful, that sounds like teasing again."

"Never, that would be bratty behaviour and you'd never catch me being bratty." She giggles.

I slap her arse hard and pull her down to rest against my chest. She snuggles in and sighs in contentment.

"Thank you, Sir." She whispers.

"What for Holly?"

"For not letting me walk away from this." Her quiet voice comes out of the darkness, her breath brushing across my chest.

"Thank you for being brave enough to come back." I kiss her hair gently.

## HOLLY

The next day is made up of fantasies and dreams, starting with breakfast in bed that ends with Bill eating fruit off different parts of my body, and licking yoghurt from my nipples. While I'm taking the required shower to remove the sticky mess from my skin, Bill joins me and pins me against the tiles.

I gasp in shock as the cold ceramic hits my heated skin, then I gasp again as Bill lifts me up and impales me on his cock in one swift move. He thrusts into me hard a fast, like a man possessed. It's fast and almost primal, and we both erupt in orgasm within minutes.

His hands hold my head still and he looks intently at me, holding my gaze for long moments.

"I love you, Holly." His words make heart flutter and swell with emotion.

"I love you too Bill." Then he just holds me close as the hot water runs over our entwined bodies.

After the intensity of our shower, Bill decides we should go for a long walk. He
takes me on what turns out to be a mini hike up a waterfall. I'm not the fittest of people and I'm out of breath by the time we get to the top, but the view is so worth the effort.

We linger for a little while watching the water cascade down into the valley bellow, and then we find a cosy little pub for a drink.

"Are you looking forward to the club later?" He asks.

"I am, it feels different today, more somehow because of our relationship, I'm excited to go there as your girlfriend not just your sub." It feels bigger somehow, more intense.

"It is different today, we've opened the door on our emotions wide and they are all coming pouring out. That's going to make our scenes a lot more intense and you're going to feel a lot more vulnerable." He takes a sip of his drink.

"That should scare me, but for some reason it doesn't."

"That's because you finally trust me to keep you safe. You can let yourself be vulnerable because you know I won't let anything happen to you."

He's right I do trust him, I should tell him about Andrew now, he will keep me safe and deal with Andrew properly. Just as I'm about to tell him everything he grabs my hand and pulls me up from my chair.

"Come on girly, time to go get ready for tonight." And just like that, the moment is gone.

I put it to the back of my mind as we drive back from the pub and get ready for the club, there will be plenty of time to tell him tomorrow. I'm just too happy to spoil it with the ugly that is Andrew.

The car park is full when we pull in, it must be really busy tonight.

"Who's manning the desk tonight?" I ask.

"Henry is doing it as an extra shift, he felt bad that I didn't have a night off when he was ill."

"That's silly, he couldn't help being ill."

"I know, but it's probably not a good idea to call a Dom silly, even if he's not your Dom." He laughs.

We reach the door and Bill holds the door open for me to enter first.

"Thank you, kind Sir." I give him a quick kiss on the lips as I walk into the reception area.

"Very nice girly, now get in there and stop Dom poking."

I'm smiling as I reach the desk where Henry is sitting.

"Someone looks in a good mood." He observes.

"She is in a good mood, good, but a bit cheeky." Bill says from behind me.

"Oh, that's definitely not a good idea when you're about to go through that door." Henry laughs.

"I think I'll be okay, he's a pussy cat really." I wink at Henry.

"Just keep poking girly, you'll get punished later." I jump in surprise as a hard slap lands on my arse.

# BILL

I smile at Henry as I follow Holly into the club room. I might be pretending to be stern, but I'm enjoying the new openness between us, Holly has relaxed so much. Since we shared our feelings there has been a new deepness and intensity, I'm looking forward to seeing how that translates into our scene.

The club room is busy, filled with the sounds of all the scenes already going on, slaps of leather against skin and shrieks of pain and pleasure. Entering the club room always fills me with excitement, the world of possibilities fires my imagination every time.

Tonight, I want to push us both further than we've ever gone before. I want to explore the new openness between us, I want to see just how deep we can go. I say hello to a few people as we make our way around the room, there is a really good crowd in tonight. The more people here, the more intense the scene, it adds a lot to the scene if she feels more vulnerable because of people watching her come apart for me.

I lead her over to the cross I have reserved for our scene, I can see she looks confused, we usually socialise for a while before we play. I want to keep her a little on edge tonight, keep her a little unbalanced so that when I push her she will cling to me as she floats into subspace.

"Strip for me Holly." I command.

"Yes Sir." She hurries to obey my order and in moments she is stood naked before me.

"Good girl, now give me your wrists." I hold my hand out palm upwards.

She looks deeply into my eyes and places her hand in mine, giving me her trust and her submission. I hold her gaze as I buckle the wrist cuffs. She takes a deep breath and I can see her relax as she lets it out again. Her head is in the right place, she has handed the control to me and she only needs to wait and feel.

Threading my hands in her hair, I pull her head back, I can see her pulse fluttering in her neck, she's excited. The connection between us is heady, the feeling is almost overwhelming. I lean towards her slowly, her lips part in anticipation of the kiss she assumes is coming. Instead I slap her arse hard.

I smile as I hear her gasp in surprise and she flinches at the sharp sting.

"Never assume you know what's coming girly, you will always be wrong." I laugh. Her expressions are so easy to read.

I back her up against the cross and clip the wrist cuffs to the rings high up, again she looks uncertain. Every time I have used the cross she has been facing it, I want her facing the room though, I want her to see anyone who stops to watch.

I can see her eyes darting around the room, and I know the exact moment she sees Gemma and Elissa, she smiles in their direction and relaxes back against the cross. Their friendly faces have had a reassuring effect on her and allowed her to submit further.

I turn around in time to see the two couples sit to watch our scene, Adam and Leo on the sofa, Elissa and Gemma knelt at their Master's feet. Turning back, I pull several toys from my bag, I hear a couple of sighs and quite a few muffled groans from Holly as she sees what I have pulled out. Of course, she is assuming I'm going to be using them all.

I know she doesn't like a couple of the toys, but the anticipation of me using them will keep her on edge nicely. I take one of the softer floggers and trail the falls over her skin, she shivers in delight at the sensation. Her nipples draw tight and peaked as her skin becomes sensitised, so I gently flog each breast in turn, then I pull my arm back and flick the flogger forward with a sharp snap.

The tips of the falls land on the peaked nipple and her groan of pleasure drifts from her lips. I alternate between soft gentle falls and sharp flicks, following a random rhythm so she never knows which is coming.

Every time a sharp flick catches her nipples, she gasps and then slides further into the scene. I know I'm going to need to work hard to get her to the point I want her at, the point where she is totally open to me, totally giving herself to my care and protection.

There always seems to be a hidden little bit of her mind that won't switch off for me, a part of herself she always protects from the world. Well tonight I am going to see all of her, I am going to have her open and vulnerable, so that I can see who she is deep down.

I exchange the flogger for the riding crop and her eyes widen in anticipation of the pain. I brush it across her nipples and then across the sensitive underside of each breast. She wriggles a little as it tickles and I fix her with a stern look.

"Don't move girly." I slap the crop against the top of her breast to reprimand her for moving.

She gasps, but doesn't move, lesson learned. I alternate between teasing her with the gentle brush of the crop and bringing it down hard against the tender skin of her breasts with a sharp crack. Her pale skin reddens with the imprint of the crop, the contrast between her almost translucent white skin and the vivid red of the crop marks is exciting.

Her head falls back against the cross and her eyes drift closed, she is finding her happy place, she is on the road to sub space.

# HOLLY

My head is floating, I am sinking so fast into sub space, I don't understand why, I've gone much further than this before and I'm usually nowhere near at this stage. The crop feels so good, everything feels so much more intense, as though our newly shared feelings have magnified every sensation.

Part of my mind is still busy though, it always is. I relax further into our scene and let my eyes drift closed. In the darkness behind my eyelids I float along with each stinging push he gives me.

"Open your eyes Holly, let me see you, all of you." His whisper sounds close to my ear.

I open my eyes and it takes me a few seconds to focus on him properly.

"There you are, you look beautiful girly. Are you relaxed now? Are you ready to really get started?" He smiles at me.

Oh fuck! He has a really sadistic gleam in his eyes. He's planning to push me further than he has before, maybe to my limits. I love pain, but I'm suddenly nervous, this might reveal more of me than I want to let people see, even Bill.

"Yes Sir." At least I think I might be.

"Good girl, close your eyes then and give everything to me."

I lean against the cross and let my eyes drift shut, pulling in a deep breath and try to relax. I gasp in surprise as he unclips my cuffs from the cross, what is he doing? Has he changed his mind? Does he not want me anymore?

"Don't look so worried girly, I'm just moving you to the bench, I have a feeling you're going to be struggling to stand up soon."

"Oh God." I hear his chuckle as his warm hands gently guide me to the spanking bench I know is off to one side.

My knees bump against the bench and his hands guide me to kneel in the position he wants me in.

"Keep your eyes closed Holly." He whispers close to my ear.

The sharp sting of a paddle slaps against my arse, making me jump at the suddenness, my head sinks back into the scene in an instant. It feels so good, the sting and the way it rushes over my skin from the place of impact until it covers my whole body. Every slap of the paddle dislodges a worry or a thought from my mind, clearing the clutter and leaving me with just feeling.

The slap of the paddle suddenly changes to the sting of the cane, my back arches as the sensation floods my mind. He starts with quick sharp blows, too fast for me to process one before the next one lands. A small flicker of panic begins as I try to process the intensity and fail.

This is almost too much sensation, he's taking me right to a line I didn't even know was there. As he delivers harder and harder blows with the cane I feel as though I am beginning to get lost in the sensation. Would I be able to find my way back? Would I be the same if I did?

The next fall of the cane pushes me off into a swirling vortex of feeling and I reach blindly for something to hold onto, my sense of panic increasing as I don't find the anchor I need. Then a strong hand grips my searching fingers, Bill, I cling to his warmth as my mind swirls. He said he would keep me safe, he will pull me back from whatever place I get lost in. The firm belief in him and the trust I have that he won't allow me to get lost unlocks my grip on reality and I spin away. I feel stripped bare in a way I never have before. Open and bare to Bill and the world, I should be scared, but because of Bill and his love I feel safe.

# BILL

Finally! There she is, she takes my breath away. Finally, she has given me her total submission and trust. The instinctive way she is clinging to my hand shows me she trusts me totally to keep her safe. I'm overwhelmed by the deep awe of such a precious gift.

The feeling that she is holding back a part of herself drifts away, I can see all of her, she's not holding anything back from me now. She has given all of herself to our relationship in a way I didn't think she ever would.

I lean down and caress her cheek.

"You're safe with me Holly, I won't let you get lost." She sighs and relaxes even further into subspace.

I can't push her much further, she has gone deep enough already, time to bring her back down and end the scene. Her eyes drift open and she looks up at me from the bench.

"My Sir!" she whispers.

"That's right Holly, I'm your Sir, and you are my beautiful little masochist." Her smile is stunning.

"I love you." She whispers as her eyes lose the battle to stay open.

Grabbing a blanket, I cover her with it and caress her back with long sweeping strokes of my hand, letting her know I am watching over her and keeping her safe while she floats around in subspace. Keeping my hand on her back to steady her I unbuckle the restraints pinning her to the bench.

Pulling her up into my arms I hold her tight, I don't want to let her go, I would be happy to hold her in my arms like this forever. The way she snuggles closer tells me she would be happy with that too. Finding a quiet area to sit, I relax onto the sofa with Holly held snugly against my chest.

A feeling of deep contentment sweeps over me as I rest my chin against her silky hair, this feeling is what I have been searching for. This is what I thought I had found with Hannah. The love I have found with Holly is so much deeper, I had to work harder for it, but it was so much deeper and intense.

Pushing thoughts of Hannah from my mind, I concentrate on the woman in my arms. My beautiful little masochist, my sub, mine!

The sounds of the club swirl around us as we sit in our own little world. I am content to sit here and watch the world go by, keeping my little masochist safe. I think all the time keeping people at arm's length were because I was waiting for the right woman to come along. Who knew she was in my club and I never knew. At least something good had come from Amy being a bitch.

Holly shifts in my arms and I hear her sigh softly, she is in a really good place, she's probably going to be out of it for a while yet. There isn't anything to rush for though. I cast a satisfied eye round all the people in the club, everyone seems to be enjoying their night.

Gemma and Leo are using the bondage table and Adam has Elissa hooked up to the whipping post. There is wax play happening over on the other side of the club and what seems to be a competition in orgasm denial going on between two Doms at the side of the dance floor.

Pure enjoyment everywhere I look, people being free to be exactly who they are and enjoy kink in their own special way.

Holly stirs in my arms and I look down to find her eyes open again.

"Hey, how are you feeling." I ask gently.

"Naked." She murmurs sleepily.

"Well that's probably because you are naked." I laugh.

"No, not that sort of naked. I mean I feel stripped bare, open and on show like I never have before. You took away my shields." Tears fill her eyes and she looks so small and vulnerable.

"You don't need shields when you are with me, just like I don't need to hide when I am with you." I smile and she smiles back.

She leans against my chest again with a contented sigh. Over by the dance floor one of the subs shrieks as her orgasm hits and her Dom groans at losing the bet with his friend. The other Dom lets out a winning cheer and the inevitable ribbing begins.

# HOLLY

The loud male laughter draws my attention and I smile at the boyish behaviour of the big bad Dom's. They all try to put on a stern appearance, but they all have this same childish sense of humour. I have a warm feeling of belonging, finally I feel as though I belong here.

I have friends, good women, and I have a man who I love and amazingly loves me back. So many good things had happened since the night I came back into the club. Mostly though it feels like I have found myself, my true self.

"What are you smiling about girly?" Bill asks, and I feel his gentle kiss on my hair.

"I'm just feeling good Sir." I'm happy, truly happy, probably for the first time.

"Then my work here is done for tonight, what shall we do now?"

"Whatever you want to do Sir."

"Oh, nicely done girly, very nice."

His approval warms me deep inside. The realisation that I want to please him dawns on me. I want to make him happy, I want to see him laugh. I reach up and touch his face, and he smiles, his cheek creasing under my hand.

"I love you Sir."

"As I love you Holly, you make me happy. Now, up you get and go to get dressed for me. I think it's time to be social." He pushes me to my feet and I stagger a little, maybe I'm not totally recovered from our scene yet.

"Careful girly, take your time." He grabs me by the waist to steady me and makes sure I am okay again before he lets go.

I find my feet and make my way over to the changing room clutching my clothes in front of me. When I push the door open, I can hear giggling coming from inside. Gemma and Elissa are getting dressed too, well they are supposed to be I think, but it looks as though they have given up all pretence of dressing and are just giggling madly at each other.

"What are you two giggling about?" They both look at me for a moment, then burst into laughter again.

Goodness knows what has made them laugh so much. Elissa waves her hands in front of her face, and it's hard to tell if she's trying to communicate or if she's having a fit. Gemma, who had almost stopped laughing starts to giggle uncontrollably again at Elissa's wild movements.

I can't help but laugh with them, even though I have no idea what they are laughing at, their laughter is contagious. There is a loud knock on the door and Leo's voice booms from the club room.

"Stop laughing and get dressed now. Don't make me come in there." He sounds annoyed, but his demand sets them both off laughing again.

I hear a muttered "Brats" from Leo outside.

"Will one of you tell me what's going on?" I try to look serious. "You two are going to be in so much trouble."

"Well, Gemma and Leo where in the middle of a scene, and he was being all masterful and impressed with himself, and then…" Elissa bursts into another fit of giggles.

"For goodness sake you two, I've seen Leo in Dom mode, it never inspires laughter."

"Okay, I'll tell you." Gemma finally has her laughter under control. "So, Leo is there being all scary Dom, and he pulls two big ass clamps out of his pocket, he'd found them in his tool box and thought it would be a good idea to try them on my nipples." She rolls her eyes and tuts.

"Well I'm still not seeing what's so funny."

"So, he's coming towards me with the clamp in his hand and that evil look on his face, he's opening and closing the clamp, trying to make it look scarier, and then, ping!" She giggles again.

"Ping?"

"Ping! The spring pinged out of the clamp and it fell apart in his hand. He looked so disappointed, like a little boy who dropped his sweets in a puddle." She explodes into laughter again.

"You know he's going to come up with something much meaner and ouchie as punishment for you laughing at him." It's never a good idea to laugh at your Dom, but especially not in the middle of a scene when his equipment fails.

"It was really funny though, the look on his face was priceless." Elissa giggles.

"Oh my, you two better hurry and get dressed, you don't want to get into even more trouble."

"Oh, I won't get into trouble, it's Gemma who's in danger." Elissa looks relieved.

"Think again little mouse." Adams voice drifts through the door. "If you don't get your arse out here fast you will be in just as much trouble as Gemma."

Elissa's smile disappears in an instant and she rushes to get dressed. I laugh at the look on both their faces, bratty is okay, but it does come back to bite you on the arse sometimes.

I join them in the rush to get dressed, not because I'm going to be in trouble like them, but just because I want to get back to Bill as soon as I can. The laughter of my friends has heightened the good feelings even more, I feel as lite as a feather, little bubbles of happiness are fizzing in my chest.

"Well will you look at that." Gemma says to Elissa gesturing towards me.

"I know, it's amazing." Elissa sighs.

"What is?" I look around behind me, trying to see what they are talking about.

"The look on your face silly." Elissa smiles at me.

"What look?"

"The happy look of a woman in love. You look all lit up inside." Gemma leans over and hugs me tight.

# BILL

The girls come out of the locker room together, laughing and giggling together like teenagers. It makes me smile, it's so good to see them together, they are all three such amazing caring women, it's great they have each other as friends.

I don't know what Gemma has been up to, but Leo is doing his best to look stern as the girls walk over to join us. I can see the amusement in his eyes though, he does love her sense of fun, and her occasional bratty behaviour.

"What did she do this time?" I ask laughing.

"Don't ask." Leo replies abruptly.

"He's feeling a little touchy about it." Adam laughs.

Oh dear, she's in trouble.

The girls kneel in front of us, heads lowered in submission. I lean forward and thread my fingers in Holly's hair, tilting her head back to look into her eyes.

"Are you feeling okay girly?"

"Yes Sir, I feel wonderful, thank you." Her face lights up with happiness.

"I love you Holly, thank you. You gave me everything in our scene, you trusted me totally to keep you safe. You gave me a huge gift." I kiss her gently.

"I love you too Sir."

I pull her up into my arms and hold her close, kissing her deeply, when I pull back, she is breathing rapidly and her pupils are dilated with arousal.

"Now off you go to sit with Gemma and Elissa, I think they have wedding planning to talk about."

"Thank you Sir, can I get you anything first?"

"No, I'm fine, but thank you for being so thoughtful." I watch as she walks over to the sofa where Gemma and Elissa are sitting, once she's sat down, I turn back to Adam and Leo.

It isn't long before they the girls are deep in conversation and we hear the words lace and chiffon being used, the wedding dress must be tonight's topic of conversation. They all look so happy and relaxed. It looks as though they are settled in for the rest of the night.

"I'm staying out of that conversation, I may be in charge, but I'm smart enough not to come between Gemma and any form of shopping." Leo laughs.

"I agree, it would take a brave man to try." Adam agrees.

"A braver one than me. Mind you her two apprentices are learning well from her. They are a powerful threesome when they get going." I add my voice full of pride. All three of them were strong, brave women who had overcome so much in their lives.

They all lend that strength to each other, making all of them stronger.

"They are stunning, aren't they?" Adam says, awe in his voice.

"They are, and you know what we are, don't you?" Leo asks.

"Damn lucky men." I answer.

"You're bloody right we are." Adam agrees.

As if she can feel my gaze, Holly looks over to me from their huddle of wedding planning. The air between us sizzles with electricity as we fall into the intensity of arousal. Holly licks her lips and I groan as I feel my cock harden.

I break the moment and look over to Adam and Leo, they are both grinning at me like fools.

"What?"

"Well, if we weren't in the club, I would be suggesting you both get a room, that was quite intense." Adam laughs.

"My feelings for Holly are intense." I tell them honestly.

"You're in love with her." Leo declares.

"Of course he is, you only need to see the looks he gives her to know that." Adam scoffs.

"I'm glad I'm so obvious and easy to read." I laugh.

"You've lost your strong silent Dom status now mate. Anyone looking at either of you can tell exactly what you both feel." Adam confirms.

"It's good to see you so happy, you've been lonely for too long." Leo looks at me with understanding, he had witnessed my worst moods after Hannah's betrayal.

"I am happy, she makes me happy." I say looking over again to where Holly is laughing with her friends.

# HOLLY

I can feel Bill's eyes on me as I try to concentrate on the wedding planning. Part of my mind is on Bill though, I can feel the connection pulling on me like an invisible thread tying us together. Something changed during our scene, when I opened myself to Bill, I let him further in at the same time.

We are connected on a much deeper level now, I'm so glad I could relax enough to let him see all of me. Suddenly I feel a need to tell him everything, I need to tell him about Andrew, I know he will believe me and he will help me deal with it. The decision suddenly feels so easy, after giving him all of myself in our scene earlier, telling him about this will be easy.

"Sorry girls, will you excuse me?" I need to talk to Bill, but first I need to visit the bathroom.

"Is everything okay Holly?" Elissa asks with a concerned look on her face.

"Yes, everything is perfect, I just need to talk to Bill." I smile.

"You're going to tell him about Andrew, aren't you?" Gemma squeezes my hand reassuringly.

"I am, it's time."

"It will be okay Holly, Bill will protect you, he loves you. Andrew needs to be sorted out, what he's doing is so wrong and he shouldn't get away with it." Gemma's temper is rising on my behalf.

"I know, I trust Bill to believe me."

I walk over and kneel on the floor in front of Bill.

"Yes girly? What do you need?" He smiles.

"Please Sir, I need to go to the bathroom, and then I need to talk to you in private."

"Are you okay Holly?" His hand caresses my face, the warmth of his skin warms me.

"Yes Sir, I just have something I need to talk to you about."

"Okay then girly, off you go to the bathroom and then we can talk."

"Thank you, Sir." I get up and make my way to the bathroom.

Once I'm done, I wash my hands and look at myself in the mirror over the sink. My hair looks like it's never been brushed and my mascara has run so much I look like a panda. I finger comb my hair and use some wet paper towel to clean my face. Once I'm presentable again I leave the bathroom to go and find Bill for our talk.

"Well look who it is, the bitch who thinks she is too good for everyone." My heart sinks, it's Andrew and from the sound of things he's been drinking.

I look around to see if there is anyone to help me, but we are in a quiet corridor away from the main room. Unless Bill comes to find me or someone needs the bathroom, there won't be any help. Hopefully he just wanted to make me feel bad and then he'll leave me alone.

"I need to get back to Bill now Andrew, please let me pass." I move to walk past him, but as I draw level with him, he grabs my arm and backs me up against the wall.

"You aren't going anywhere until I say you can. I told you we would scene again didn't I?" I can smell the alcohol on his breath and it turns my stomach.

"Andrew, let me go, you're drunk and this is wrong. You know it's wrong." I hope he's not too drunk to reason with.

"I don't care, you've brushed me off for the last time." He leans against me, pushing me harder against the wall. I can feel his erection pressing against me. I look wildly about for someone to help me, but the corridor is deserted.

"Be sensible Andrew. You know you can't get away with this."

"Oh, I think I can, who's going to believe you over me." He leans down and kisses me, forcing his tongue into my mouth. I squirm wildly, trying to push him away, but he just laughs.

"Bill will come looking for me, he will believe me." I say confidently, I know he will.

"Are you sure about that? He doesn't like people who lie." He laughs.

"I haven't lied to him, and yes I'm sure he will believe me."

"You didn't tell him, though did you? That's as bad as lying."

He has a point, but I trust Bill, he has told me over and over that he will protect me, I have to believe him.

I struggle again to break free of his hold, but he's too strong for me. I try to knee him in the crotch, but he pins my leg against the wall with his knee. I can't get free, no matter how hard I try, my only hope now is that Bill will come looking for me.

# BILL

Holly has been gone a while, I decide to meet her on her way back from the bathroom, we can go to the flat to talk. I have no idea what she wants to talk about, but I hope it's something good. Today has been a good day, I think Holly is ready to commit fully to our relationship.

Whatever it was that has been bothering her seems to have passed, she has been much more relaxed over the last couple of weeks. I'm surprised I haven't found her yet, how long does it take a woman to pee anyway?

As I turn into the corridor, I feel a strange sense of de-ja-vu. Thoughts of the night I found Hannah with another man flash through my mind, and I shake my head to brush them away. The past shouldn't be intruding on my present.

The sight that hits me once I turn the corner feels like a ten-ton truck has just slammed into my chest. It steals my breath, and I don't seem to be able to pull in another one. Holly, my Holly is pinned up against the wall in a passionate embrace with Andrew.

So, this is what she wanted to talk to me about, her extracurricular activities. Well, if she thinks I'm willing to share she has another thing coming. I won't share with anyone, especially not someone like Andrew. I remember my uneasy feelings about him from a few weeks ago, why hadn't I looked at him more closely?

I'd thought Holly was different, I never thought she would be exactly the same as Hannah.

"Well, well, well, what have we here? Is this a private party or can anyone join in?" I sneer.

Andrew takes his time turning to look at me, arrogant bastard.

"Oh, look who it is sweetheart, it's your other man. I don't feel like letting him join in though, do you?"

Holly gasps and turns her tear stained face to me.

"Bill." There is a note of pleading in her voice, but I close my heart to it. I'm not falling for her lies any longer.

"I take it this is what you were going to talk to me about, well there's no need now is there, I already know."

"Bill, please, it's not like that."

"Now pet, don't pretend, Bill can see how it is, he understands how things like this go." Andrew leans over and kisses her neck.

"I do understand. Don't worry I'll leave you two alone. Holly I thought we had something good, obviously I was wrong. I don't want to see you in my club again, you need to find somewhere else to play with people."

I turn away and walk away, back through the club. I'm almost at the door to my flat when Adam catches up with me.

"What's wrong with you? Where's Holly?" He grabs my arm to stop my progress.

"I'm done with Holly, in fact I'm done with women full stop. You can't trust a single one of them. I'd rethink the whole marriage thing if I were you, she's probably just waiting for the chance to get in some other poor fool's pants."

In some part of my brain I know I just crossed a line, but my anger is in control now not my head.

"You didn't just go there, Bill do you have a death wish? What the hell happened, you were all loved up half an hour ago." I can see Adam is close to losing his temper.

"It doesn't matter what happened."

"It does when it makes you attack my fiancé for no other reason that she is a woman." Adam lets go of my arm and takes a step away from me.

"I need to be on my own." I turn to open the door.

"No, you need to calm down and tell me what's going on." He grabs my arm again and I turn instinctively with my fist clenched, and punch Adam in the jaw. He lets go of my arm and I leave his spluttering behind me as I storm into my flat and slam the door shut.

Finally, I am alone, I can deal with what just happened and sort my head out, my heart? Well that was another matter.

# HOLLY

He left! He didn't even give me a chance to ask for his help, he just assumed I was cheating on him and left. The pain cut's through me like a knife, Andrew was right then, people would believe him over me.

Another realisation dawns, now no one is coming to help me, Andrew will do whatever he likes and I'm not strong enough to stop him. Tears begin to fall freely, and a sob escapes.

"Oh, don't cry pet. I told you this would happen, didn't I?" He laughs.

"Let me go now." I demand.

"You are in no position to make demands, you are the sub, you'll do as you are told, which will be exactly what I want." He leans down to kiss me again, but I'm ready for him this time. I may not be able to reach his crotch with my knee, but I can reach his foot with my heels.

I lift my foot as high as I can and ram my heel down onto the top of his foot.

"You little bitch." He shouts, and slaps me hard across my left cheek. Pain slams into me and black dots float in my vision.

I must have let out a cry, but I didn't hear it. All I can hear is the ringing in my ears. He pulls his hand back to hit me again and I close my eyes and brace myself for the pain I know is coming.

It never comes though, instead I hear a thud. I open my eyes to see Gemma and Elissa standing in front of me and Andrew lying on the floor. Gemma has a plant pot in her hand and Andrew is unconscious and covered in soil.

"Holly, are you okay?" Elissa reaches her arms out to me, but I back away, I don't want anyone touching me just now. It feels as though one little fingertip touch will be enough to shatter me into millions of pieces.

"Holly it's okay, it's over, you're safe now." Gemma says softly.

I'm not alone, my friends came to help me, not Bill though, he left me on my own.

I can feel myself begin to tremble, and in the space of a few seconds I am shaking so much my teeth are chattering.

"She's going into shock, she needs a blanket." I hear Leo say from the entrance to the corridor.

He steps closer and holds out a fluffy blanket to Gemma. I shrink back against the wall, still trembling and shaking.

"It's okay Holly, I'm not going to come any closer, I'm just going to remove this mess from the club." He smiles gently at me and bends to grab a waking Andrew by the arm. He drags him away and around the corner out of sight.

Gemma comes closer to me and wraps the blanket around my shoulders. Her arms pull me closer and I hesitate for a few seconds before I collapse against her and great heaving sobs break free.

"It's okay Holly, it's over, we're here and you're safe." She murmurs against my hair.

"Where is Bill? Should we go and let him know what happened?" Elissa asks softly, her hands stroking my back in long calming strokes.

"He knows. He was here and he left." I say with a huge gulp of tears.

"What do you mean he left, could he not see what was happening?" I can hear the anger in Gemma's voice.

"He thinks I was cheating on him with Andrew. He took one look and decided that's what was going on. I asked him to help me and he just walked away, he told me he would always protect me, that I could count on him, but he just turned away and left me."

"We need to explain to him." Elissa whispers.

"He shouldn't need an explanation, he should trust Holly and protect her, not walk away and leave her being attacked." Gemma is in full flow now.

"We should get you home Holly." Elissa says.

"Not yet I'm afraid." It's Adam.

"Adam, she is in shock and she needs quiet and rest." She argues.

"The police are on their way, she needs to talk to them before she goes home, this isn't just a consent violation, this was attempted rape and assault." I look up and gasp in shock as I see the bruise forming along Adam's jaw.

"Adam, what happened to your face?" Had Andrew hit Adam too?

"Bill punched me." He says wryly.

"No, way? What is wrong with him?" Gemma gasps.

"He's not thinking, he's just reacting. His view is coloured by his past." Adam explains.

"His past is no excuse, he should have dealt with Andrew, not walked away and left Holly to be attacked."

"Hey, I'm not excusing what he did, I'm just saying that's why he did it. He's being an idiot and he's let Holly down badly."

"The police are here honey, lets go into the office and you can get this over with." Leo appears at the entry to the corridor.

"Where is Andrew?" I don't want to see him.

"He's already outside in the police car sweetie, you don't need to go anywhere near him." Leo reassures me.

Gemma and Elissa both wrap their arms round me and lead me to the office where the police are waiting for me. The hold my hands as I explain all about Andrews intimidation over the last few months leading up to his attack tonight. Then, once the police are finished asking their endless questions, they take me home and run me a hot bath.

Once I'm lying in my bed, they sit with me as the tears flow and my heart breaks all over again. This was the reason I only count on myself, that way no one lets you down. Bill had promised me he would protect me, he would help me deal with anything. The first time I needed him he just walked away.

He hadn't believed in me, when it came down to it, his past counted more than I did.

# BILL

I wake up the next morning with the hangover from hell. I had switched off from everything by getting stinking drunk. Now I was paying the price, not only was all the hurt from Holly's betrayal still there, but now it had been joined by a pounding head and upset stomach.

How could I have been so wrong about her? Last night she had seemed so open with me, was my judgement so off that I misread her? Why had she said she loved me when she so obviously didn't? The image of her and Andrew locked in a passionate embrace keeps flashing through my head.

I need water, at least I can do something about the hangover. I head to the kitchen and fill a glass with icy cold water, I'm just downing my second glass full when there is a loud pounding on the door.

Who the hell is this? I really don't want to see anyone, I want to wallow in my own pain and deal with my hangover. The pounding begins again even louder, but this time it's accompanied by a very angry female voice.

"Bill you open this door right now." It's a very pissed off Gemma, just what I don't need this morning.

"Go away Gemma, I really don't want to see anyone." I saw wearily.

"Tough shit mister. I'm going to stay here till you let us in."

"You might as well give in you know, she's got that look in her eye, I don't think she's going to give up." Leo shouts through the door.

I walk to the door and pull it open with a sharp yank revealing a small crowd on my door step.

Leo and Gemma, Adam and Elissa, all looking at me like I'm an axe murderer.

"Really guys, I'm not up to a post mortem on last night, I just want to be left alone." I'm too tired to deal with this.

"Well that's just not happening is it?" Gemma pushes past me into the flat, followed by Leo then Elissa.

As Adam draws level with me, I see the darkening bruise along his jaw, a deep feeling of guilt fills me. I definitely shouldn't have hit Adam.

"I'm sorry Adam, I should never have hit you. I let my temper get the better of me and I was wrong."

"Yes, it was wrong, I've never seen you lose your control like that, even after Hannah."

Shame fills me, how could I lose control like that? As a Dom I prided myself on my control, I never scened if I was angry or in a bad mood. All it had taken was another betrayal by a woman to have me turning on my friend.

"I'm sorry Adam." I really can't say anything else. There aren't any excuses.

"I know you are, but you'll find being sorry for hitting me is small in comparison to the thing you should really be sorry for." He pushes me ahead of him into the lounge where the rest of the group are waiting.

Gemma is bristling with anger and indignation. Leo's arm is holding her back, but it looks as though it's hard work.

"Calm down a bit sweetheart." He says.

She takes a deep breath and lets it out in a big sigh.

"You're right, I need to calm down a bit." She smiles at him, when she turns to me her face is cold though.

"What the hell am I supposed to have done, apart from punch Adam that is? I'm the one she cheated on you know. Just because she's your friend doesn't mean you automatically need to take her side." It hurts that my friends would turn against me.

"What have you done? Oh my god, you have no idea, do you?" I'm surprised by the amount of venom in Elissa's voice. She is usually so quiet and timid.

She turns to Adam with a questioning look.

"Oh, go to it little mouse." He laughs.

"No punishment?" she asks.

"No, you can give it to him both barrels, Dom or no Dom." He says.

Elissa turns to Gemma and smiles.

"You too sweetheart." Leo whispers in Gemma's ear.

"What's going on here?" I'm confused now.

"Well since you are so dense that you have no idea what happened last night, we'll tell you." Gemma says.

"Andrew has been putting pressure on Holly since she came back to the club, he's been pressuring her to scene with him, we interrupted him once when he had hold of her by the arm." Elissa explains.

"He went to her work, outed her to her boss, tried to get her fired." Gemma spits at me.

"If that's true, then why didn't she tell me?" They have to be wrong.

"Because, you bloody idiot, she's been so used to standing on her own two feet for so long, that she's forgotten how to depend on anyone. Add that to the fact Andrew told her he would tell you she was cheating on you if she didn't scene with him." Gemma is really getting into full flow now.

"She was worried everyone would believe him over her, that because of what happened with Amy she had caused enough trouble and upset in the club."

"Well, she was right wasn't she." Gemma snaps.

"I would have known if all that was going on under my nose." I definitely can't have missed that.

"Really? You think? You didn't do a good job of seeing what was going on last night did you?" Elissa shouts.

She steps closer to me and punctuates her next words with a jab of her finger in my chest.

"Andrew was trying to rape her you bloody blind bastard."

The bottom falls out of my world as her words sink in.

"No!"

"Yes, she was trying to fight him off, when you came, she thought she was safe because you said you loved her, you promised you would protect her. Then the first time she needs your protection and safety, you fucking walk away and leave her alone." Tears are streaming down Gemma's cheeks.

"She pleaded with you to help her, but you turned your back on her and left. Then when Adam tried to find out what was wrong, you hit him." Elissa is also crying.

"I had to do what you wouldn't do. I knocked him out and helped Holly. The woman you said you loved, the woman you left all alone." Gemma turns and walks out, leaving me in the centre of my shattered world.

# HOLLY

Friday night comes around far too quickly, my heart is breaking all over again. I've not only lost Bill, I've lost the club too. This week has been the stuff of nightmares, I had to give an official statement the morning after Andrew attacked me. Sunday was the longest day I've ever lived through.

I cried, I slept, I got really angry at both men. Gemma and Elissa had stayed with me all day, in the end I pretended to be asleep so they would go home. I just wanted to be alone, find a way to deal with all this by myself.

When I walked into work on Monday morning Jackson immediately called me into his office. He wanted to know what was wrong, it's nice to know it's so obvious something is wrong. He was so supportive and sympathetic that I burst into tears in the middle of his office and he had to send me home.

I had taken two days off, until I couldn't stand my own company any longer so I went back to work. I was just going through the motions of living. I felt numb inside, like I had shut down. The police had given me regular updates, I was really surprised by how accepting they were of the scene, I had expected them to say it was my own fault.

I really don't know what I'm going to do now. When I had gone back to the club to apologise to Elissa, my intention had been to walk away from the scene. Since then though I had found what the scene was really like and I had got so much deeper into it.

How was I going to walk away from it all now? At least I would still see my friends without having to go into the club. We still have a wedding to plan after all. I don't think I can go to the engagement party though, it's just too soon. By the time the wedding comes around I might be feeling a bit braver.

Bill hadn't been in touch at all, not that I'm surprised, he made his feelings pretty clear when he walked away. How could you do that to someone you supposedly love? I know I should have told him about Andrew sooner, but he still should have believed me, or at least given me a chance to explain.

The fact that I was on the way to tell him all about it when it all fell apart just makes it harder to accept. Would it have made a difference if I had told him from the beginning? It's hard to say, if I'd told him at the beginning, he probably wouldn't have believed me because he didn't know me very well, but once we had got closer who knows?

His judgement was obviously still influenced by what Hannah had done, nothing I could have said to him in that corridor would have changed his mind. I can still see the look on his face, disbelief, closely followed by such intense anger. He had made up his mind based totally on his past experience.

In the end his words had meant nothing, all his promises of love and protection were empty, when I had needed him the most, he had turned his back on me and walked away without a backward glance.

I always knew I only had myself to rely on, this has just proved it to me. I just wish I didn't feel like I have lost such a huge part of myself. I had opened myself to him totally, laid myself bare for him to see everything. My every feeling and emotion had been there for him to see, and he had taken me there, broken through my walls and then he had abandoned me, leaving me to deal with Andrew on my own.

In the space of a few hours I had gone from deep feelings of love and happiness, through to total vulnerability and nakedness, finally ending up at heartbreak and despair. My body feels battered and I'm so tired, yet I can't seem to sleep.

More than once this week I have sat for a few minutes and realised hours later that I am still sat there staring off into space. Gemma and Elissa have come to see me more than once, their hugs of comfort and sympathy are lovely, but they aren't the hugs I'm craving.

I don't want to need him, but I do, I still want him. At least my need for him gives me my answer about the club, I can't go back in there, I can't see Bill again that would just be too painful. Add to that the fact that all the people who had been so disapproving of me when I had first come back in to the club would revert back to the same opinion, and the club is lost to me.

The tears I thought had finally run out begin to flow again.

## BILL

Banging on my door hits my ears and booms through my brain like a cannon being fired. Who the hell is that? I'd told everyone to leave me alone. I need time to wallow in my anger at myself, at my own stupidity.

The banging gets louder and I pull myself up off the sofa, as I stand up, I stagger at the stab of pain through my skull. Whoever this is better have a really good excuse for banging on my door. Yanking the door open with an angry "WHAT!" I find Gemma stood outside rubbing her sore knuckles.

"Don't ever make me knock that hard on a door again. If my knuckles bruise Leo will be looking for you." She grumbles.

"How is it my fault if you bruise your knuckles abusing my front door?" I'm confused.

"If you hadn't got your head stuck up your own arse, I wouldn't need to be here banging on your door, would I?" She barges past me into the lounge.

"Gemma, I really don't have the energy for this, I have a headache." I pinch the bridge of my nose to try and relieve the pressure.

"Well that's what you get when you go on a seven-day drinking binge, isn't it? Do you expect me to be sympathetic?"

"No, I expect you to leave me alone." I snap.

"Well we all have hopes and dreams, don't we? They don't always come true though. I'm sure Holly had dreams of being with you for a long time, but that didn't happen either did it?"

"Gemma, I know I fucked up, if you've come here just to tell me again, there's really no need, I've been beating myself up for it all week." I walk into the kitchen to find something to take for this headache.

"How's that working out for you Bill?" She's right behind me as I pour myself some water to take the paracetamol with.

"Just fine Gemma, or it would be if people would leave me alone."

"Bill, you and Holly love each other, you need to sort this out." She touches my arm sympathetically.

"This can't be sorted out Gemma, leave it alone." There is no coming back from this, I let her down and in the worst way possible.

"I think it can. She loves you Bill, do you love her?"

"Of course I love her, but she won't ever forgive me for this and I really can't blame her."

"So, you're just going to give up then?" She challenges.

"What other choice do I have Gemma? I let her down, I walked away and left her alone while she was being attacked, how can we ever move past that?"

"Well, that depends on if you can ever get over what Hannah did to you. Holly deserves all of you and all of your trust. You've spent so much time and energy uncovering the inner Holly, but you should have been dealing with your own issues at the same time."

"So, what would you suggest I do now?"

"Look inside Bill, claim back the part of you that Hannah stole, claim it back and then give it to Holly."

"What if I can't find it? What if Holly doesn't want it if I do?"

"You will find it Bill, it's almost there, if you'd had more time you would have been more confident in her and it all would have been fine, but Andrew decided he would put a stop to that."

"Why are you being nice to me now? You were ready to punch me last week."

"Because I happen to think you're a pretty good guy, despite you being a total idiot last week, and because Holly is my friend and I want to see her happy."

"You think I can make her happy, do you really think she might still give me a chance?"

"That all depends on Holly really, and on how good you are at apologising. Can you be as brave as Holly was when she came into the club to apologise to Elissa?"

Gemma was right, Holly had been brave, she had come into the club because apologising was the right thing to do, not the easy thing, but the right thing. I need to do the right thing and apologise to her, publicly, whether she wants me back or not.

"You're right Gemma."

"I know, I quite often am. Well, my work here is done, I have things to do and a party to plan."

She walks towards the front door with her usual burst of energy.

"Gemma!" I call out as she opens the door.

"Yes?"

"Thank you." I didn't deserve her advice or kindness.

"You're welcome, don't make me regret it." She walks out of the door, but turns at the last minute. "For goodness sake crack a window in here and take a shower, you smell like a stale beer barrel."

# HOLLY

"More wine Holly?" Elissa asks.

"I shouldn't, I have work tomorrow." Not that I felt like going in.

"Go on, you look like you need to unwind a bit more." Gemma smiles at me.

Well that isn't really going to happen, I haven't properly relaxed since Andrews attack in the club. I've had the stress of visits from the police and reliving the attack when I gave my formal statement, the stress when they told me he was out on bail, wondering if he would start his intimidation again. Thankfully, he has kept away and left me alone.

"Do you need to talk?" Elissa asks as she tops up Gemma's glass then hovers over mine.

"I think I'm all talked out, there's nothing left to say really." It's over, that's all there is to it.

"Has Bill still not been in touch?" Gemma looks sympathetic.

"No, why would he? He made his choice when he walked away. He doesn't want me, I was just a fling I suppose."

"Oh Holly, no that's not right, he loves you, I know he does." Elissa cries out.

"Well, he had a funny way of showing it."

"He knows he fucked up Holly, his head was in his past with Hannah." Gemma says, as if I don't know that already.

"If I am with someone, I want them with me totally, I don't want to compete with someone from their past. I'm worth more than that."

"You definitely are, and he was definitely wrong, but I know just how much things that happened in the past can affect the way you see things in the present. It can make you see things that aren't there and it can make you close yourself off from what could be something amazing." Elissa says softly, I can see tears in her eyes.

"This is different."

"Why? Because Bill is a man? That doesn't mean he can't be hurt just as much as a woman can." Elissa says.

"Neither of you were around when Hannah left, it was awful. She had been cheating on him for months when he found them. He shut down for a long time afterwards, he didn't move from the front desk, he didn't play with anyone, he didn't go out. He was a mess, I've never seen him like that before, or since, until this week." Gemma explains.

"But I didn't cheat on him."

"I know that, and so does he now, but all he could see at the time was Hannah and what she did."

"It doesn't matter now, he should have trusted me."

"Like you should have trusted him? You should have trusted him enough to tell him about Andrew." Gemma's words hit me right in the centre of my chest and knock the air out of me. She's right, I should have trusted him, but when it came down to it, he hadn't done what he said he would do.

"Well like I said it doesn't matter now. We need to get busy planning this party." In truth the party planning was the only thing keeping me going at the moment.

"Did you speak to Sophie yet? Is she coming down for the party?" Gemma asks.

"I did, she's coming down early so we can spend some time together." Elissa beams at us.

"How long is it since you've seen her?" I ask.

"It's been a while, I hadn't seen her for months and months before I moved here, then Adam helped us reconnect and I've seen her a couple of times, but she's been busy finishing her degree, so we haven't been able to get together."

"How old is she? Gemma said she's younger than you."

"She's twenty-two, so quite a lot younger than me."

I know Elissa's childhood was hard, her Mother was awful apparently and had treated Elissa a lot differently than she had Sophie. That is why the Sister's had drifted apart and hadn't seen each other for so long. Elissa had thought Sophie knew how their Mother treated her, but she had only found out after Elissa had left home.

"Does she know about the club and what you two are into?"

"Yes, I told her the last time she came to stay, although I think she already had her suspicions."

"Was she okay with it, or totally freaked out?"

"I would say she was more than a little intrigued by the idea, a little too intrigued." She laughs.

"Oh, my sister totally freaked out when I told her." Gemma laughs, "She almost ran screaming from the room."

"Oh no!"

"It's okay now, she takes the stance that if it makes me happy then great, but she has no need to hear about it."

"That's probably safest." I laugh.

"Okay team, lets get back to the planning." Gemma is all business now.

We spend the next few hours going over the final preparations for the engagement party. The fine details take my mind off the deep sadness and hurt losing Bill. He might have let me down badly, but God I miss him.

"Now we only need to decide what we are all wearing, the weather forecast is looking good, do we think dresses or something warmer?" Gemma looks excited, I can almost hear her mentally planning a shopping trip.

"I think you both need dresses, I mean if it ends up being a bit cool you could always have a wrap."

"Good idea, wait a minute, what do you mean both of us need dresses? What are you planning to wear?" Gemma pins me with a determined look.

"I will probably be in my pyjamas on my sofa." I laugh.

I hear a gasp from Elissa.

"What do you mean? Why aren't you coming to my party?" Oh no, I had been afraid of this, I can hear the hurt in her voice.

"Elissa, I can't. I'm assuming Bill will be there and I can't see him, it would be too painful."

"I could ask him not to come."

"No, you can't do that, Adam has known Bill for a long time, he should be here rather than me, if only one of us is coming."

"You are my friend, you are helping me plan the party, you have to come."

"At least think about it, it's still a couple of weeks away, you might feel differently about it by then." Gemma suggests.

"Okay, I promise to think about it." That's the best I can do.

# BILL

How can I ever make this up to her? I have no idea, the likelihood of her ever accepting my apology is slim, let alone forgiving me for it. Not that I blame her in the slightest, I had made her open herself to me, give me her trust and then I had shattered it just hours later.

I don't deserve to be forgiven, I definitely don't deserve her trust. She does deserve my apology though. If she could be brave enough to apologise to Elissa, then I should definitely man up and apologise for letting her down so badly.

Picking up my phone, I dial her number and hold my breath, would she even speak to me? The phone rings a few times and then abruptly cuts off to the voicemail message. I try again and it doesn't even ring before it hits the voicemail. As I feared she isn't going to speak to me.

I type a text message asking her to let me talk to her and hit send. Only silence greets me. Maybe if I go to her house and try to speak to her in person it would be better, but the last thing I want to do is put any pressure on her.

I need some advice, but who can I ask for it? Most people would take the opportunity to make jokes and have a good laugh at the Dom needing advice. I have to apologise to her, tell her how incredibly sorry I am for not trusting her when I demanded that she trust me.

Maybe Adam or Leo would be the best people to ask for advice, or even both of them. They are both happy and in love, they must be doing something right. Gemma and Elissa always look happy, of course neither of them looked too happy with me last week, I've never seen Elissa so angry, she is normally so timid and quiet.

The girls had really taken to Holly, she was definitely part of the group now, it really is amazing after the history between her and Elissa. Elissa had done much better job of moving on from her past than I had. The engagement party isn't long away, maybe I can talk to Holly there if she still hasn't answered my calls.

I go through the motions of the day job, stocking the bar and cleaning the club, but my mind is on Holly. I have let my own insecurities cost me the love of my life, she had given me a part of myself back that I thought I had lost forever, and how have I repaid her? By abandoning her just when she needed me most.

The police had been to ask me some questions of course, I had answered their questions, but I hadn't missed the disapproving look on the officer's face when I told him I had walked away. Every time I talk about it, it sounds worse and worse. The police had told me some of what Andrew had been doing, I can't believe Holly had felt she needed to deal with this alone, but then I had just proved to her that she did.

She must hate me right now, but she can't possibly hate me more than I do myself. I will never forgive myself for this, and because of that, I can't expect her to either.

My phone rings as I'm cleaning down the play areas and I rush to answer it, hoping that it might be Holly. It's not.

"Hey Adam." Disappointment colours my tone.

"Well don't sound so pleased to hear from me." He laughs.

"Sorry Adam, I was hoping it was Holly."

"I know you were. Have you tried to contact her yet?" He asks.

"I have, but she isn't answering my calls. Not that I blame her."

"Well, no neither can I really."

"Was there something else you wanted, apart from making me feel worse than I already do?" I ask irritated.

"There was indeed, Leo suggested we all meet up to discuss your strategy for making things up to Holly."

"I don't think there is anything I can do, nothing can make up for what I did."

"Leo has an idea, you'll need to park your Dominant tendencies though, do you think you can do that?"

"I will try anything to get Holly back, I love her."

"Okay, we're at the pub waiting for you, don't take too long."

"I'm on my way." At this point I'm open to any suggestions.

"Oh, and Bill."

"Yes?"

"I will think of something really good for you to make up for my bruised jaw." Adam hangs up laughing.

## HOLLY

I'm late for my shopping trip with Elissa and Gemma, they both want help choosing dresses for the engagement party, although I've never known Gemma need help with anything relating to shopping before. I sense a plot to get me to agree to attend the party.

Elissa has tried to guilt me into saying I'll go, Gemma has been rather bossy about it, especially for a sub. Now I think they are trying trick me into it, that or they have decided to team up and work on me at the same time.

The last week has been awful, I'm so exhausted, I keep bursting into tears for the smallest reasons, I'm not sleeping, and I really miss Bill. It's not helping that I'm beginning to crave the peace that I get from the pain of a good impact scene.

The thought of doing a scene with anyone but Bill makes me feel sick though. I'm late now because I had sat staring off into space for so long thinking about him, longing for him. I miss his laughter, I miss his arms around me, I miss the love I thought we had.

I walk into the shopping centre and look around for the girls. I spot them sitting in the coffee shop talking to a much younger girl. This must me Elissa's Sister, I can see the resemblance even though she is quite a bit younger than Elissa.

"Finally! Where have you been?" Gemma's voice is loud enough to turn heads in the whole of the coffee shop.

I can feel a blush creep over my skin as I'm suddenly the focus of so much attention.

"Sorry, I lost track of time." I mumble as I sit at the table.

"Holly, you look awful." Gemma exclaims.

"Gemma, that's hardly helpful." Elissa says shocked.

"I only speak the truth." Gemma smiles gently at me.

"I know I look bad, trust me I feel even worse."

"Honey, are you sleeping? You look so tired." Elissa takes hold of my hand and holds tight.

"No, I'm really not. I can't get the image of Bills face just as he walked away out of my mind." I can feel the tears fill my eyes.

"Has he been in touch?" Gemma's tone says he better have been.

"He's tried calling a couple of times and he sent a few text messages, but I haven't answered him."

"You miss him though."

"I do, I miss him so much it hurts, but I need to be loved a hundred percent, I can't be in a relationship with Bill if I don't have all of him. I gave him everything, and it still wasn't enough."

"Maybe he wants to apologise?" Elissa says hopefully.

"After hearing what he did it would take more than an apology to get me to listen to him." Sophie says.

"I know why he did it though, I know it came from a place of hurt, it just hurt me too much to forget."

"You sound much more forgiving than I would be." Sophie shakes her head.

"Not forgiving exactly, just understanding." I laugh ruefully.

I really need all of the man I'm with, not the bits left over from his life with someone else.

"I want you to come to the party. Bill won't be one of the guests attending." Elissa pleads.

"I told you not to do that. Bill has been Adam's friend longer than I have been yours, if anyone should come it's him." I cry.

"We didn't exclude him." She says looking a bit embarrassed.

"Well it doesn't matter either way, look Holly, you need to be there and I'm not taking no for an answer." Gemma joins in.

I can see the determination in her eyes.

"Is there any point in me arguing?" I ask in exasperation.

"Not really no." Gemma smiles sweetly at me.

I sigh and look at Sophie who is laughing quietly.

"I think you might just need to give up." She smiles at me.

"It looks like it." I smile back.

"Okay, now that's sorted I think it's time we went dress shopping, don't you?" Gemma says.

## BILL

The weekend rolls around again, but I don't have any interest in leaving the front desk and venturing into the club room.

I'm still thinking about Leo's idea to win Holly back. It sounds a bit of a long shot to me, but at this point I'm ready to try anything. After the early evening rush, I sit at the desk with a blank piece of paper in from of me, trying to decide what I could possibly write.

I've been trying to find the right words for days now, but everything I come up with seems shallow or just too cheesy. If I can't find the right words I may as well give up. I write a greeting, and then cross it out again.

I sigh in exasperation, this is just too hard, but it is my penance, my only way of telling Holly just how sorry I am.

"You sound like you have the weight of the world on your shoulders." Henry says walking up to the desk.

"Just the weight of guilt." I say shaking my head.

"Oh, heavier than the world then." He smiles.

"Just a bit."

"So, what are you trying to write? An apology letter?"

"Something like that, yes."

"Never easy to write, but especially not when you know you've really fucked up."

"Thanks for that Henry." I say sarcastically.

"Look, it's simple really, just put yourself on the page, be honest and tell her exactly how you feel."

"You say that as though it's easy."

"If you love her it should be."

"It never has been for me, and it's been even worse since Hannah, now I have destroyed something amazing because I was a coward."

"Then grow a pair and make it right." He says sharply.

"Just say it like it is, why don't you"

"Look, you may be older than me, and you may have had lots more experience, but you really are clueless. Holly is so good for you, anyone could see how much she loves you, and you have the same love for her."

"After what I did, I'm not sure that will be enough."

"True love always wins in the end." He smiles gently at me.

"This isn't a fairy tale Henry, it's real life."

"I know, and that's what makes it so important. Life is too short not to give it your all every second of every day." He shakes his head and walks away from the desk into the club.

I look down at the blank page again, put pen to paper and start writing. Everything I hadn't been able to say to her flowed through my pen and onto the paper. All my love and my fears, my hopes and dreams. My regret and self-disgust over what happened.

This letter is my one chance to get her back and I am pouring my soul into it. If this fails then everything is lost.

## HOLLY

The party is only a few days away now, I still can't believe that Elissa and Gemma tricked me into going. At least Bill won't be there, although it's still sad that he hasn't been invited now because of me. I will just have to try my hardest not to create a dark cloud of sadness over Elissa's day.

She had looked radiant in the dress she had chosen on our shopping trip, all she could think of was how pleased Adam would be when he saw her in it. She tried very hard not to be self-conscious these days. I get a sense though that she had a lot more confidence in herself now than she had the first time I saw her in the club.

Her Sister was lovely too, Elissa had been so nervous about her coming to stay, but it looked like they were getting on well. Elissa had explained to me how, because of their Mother, they hadn't got on well. Their Mother sounded like a very disturbed woman, no wonder Elissa had the issues she did.

My Mum and Dad had been wonderful, which made it all that much harder when I lost them so soon. I'm very much like Elissa in some respects, although for different reasons, both of us longed for someone to be there for us, someone to look after us and love us.

Elissa had found her soul mate, I had thought I had found mine. I know Bill loves me though, that's the silly part of all this. I know that deep down he really loves me, the same way I love him, his love just wasn't enough to overcome his distrust.

I shake my head sadly as I go to get ready for lunch with the girls. We had last minute party planning to do. Gemma was determined to make this the most magical party for Elissa and Adam. I had thought we would need to rein her in a little, but she had been remarkably restrained and tasteful.

I'm the first to arrive at the restaurant, and I read the menu while I'm waiting for the others. I decide what I'm going to order just as they arrive with a flurry of energy and hugs.

"You look better today." Elissa says.

"It's an illusion." I laugh.

"No, you look calmer, less like you are about to burst into tears." She leans over and hugs me tight.

"I've been doing a lot of thinking, I might still be hurt by what Bill did, but at least I understand why he did it. I'm just braver than him."

"Did you just call Bill the Sadist a coward?" Gemma laughs loudly.

"I did, it takes bravery to trust someone and he didn't, now I understand why he didn't, but that's not my issue, that's his issue. Unless he can sort it out in his head, he'll never fully open his heart to someone."

"Do you think he ever will?" Sophie asks.

"I hope he does, he deserves someone good."

"So do you." Gemma says sharply.

"I do, that's why I could never settle for less." I am determined never to settle for less, I'd rather be alone than settle.

"Maybe Bill will come to his senses and realise that he needs you." Elissa says gently.

"Or maybe not."

The conversation turns to the party and Elissa's wedding plans, it's wonderful to see her so happy and in love.

"I've never seen her look like this before." Sophie leans over and whispers to me.

"Like what?"

"Happy! It's like she's all lit up inside, but it's more than that. She looks like she is happy with who she is, finally she looks like she loves herself." There are tears glistening in Sophie's eyes.

"She is such a lovely person, she deserves to be happy and Adam is so in love with her."

"He is, I wasn't sure about all this BDSM stuff when she told me about it, but it's definitely changed Elissa, brought out her confidence."

"She told you then?" I can't decide if I'm surprised or not.

"They both did, they sat me down and explained it all to me. Not in graphic detail you understand." She laughs.

"Eww I hope not, no one wants to imagine their Sister doing sex stuff." I shudder.

"Tell me though, Gemma said Bill is a Sadist, is Adam one too?" She looks concerned.

"Well that is probably something you should ask Adam and Elissa, it's not really the done thing to talk about someone else's kink preferences."

"I suppose it is rude. I just wondered what anyone gets out of being in pain."

"Well, I can answer that for you. I am a masochist so I can try and explain it to you."

"So, you actually like being in pain?"

"That depends on the pain." I laugh "If I stub my toe on the bed I still swear and cry."

"So, what makes this different?" She looks confused.

"It's different because I am in a different mind-set, I'm expecting the pain, I'm ready for it, I'm craving the feel of it, once I get in that mind set, I can enjoy the pure sensation of pain without all the added thoughts that usually run through my head. The pain washes everything else away and just leaves pure feeling." I don't know if I am explaining it in a way she can understand, I don't even understand it myself.

"That's what happens to me when I paint, I get lost in the action od the brush strokes, and the image it's creating, there isn't room for any other thoughts or worries, it's such a peaceful place." I can hear the excitement in her voice.

"Yes, that's exactly how it is. I didn't know you were an artist."

"I only paint for myself now, I couldn't find a job that included my art, so I just work in retail for now." She looks sad.

"What sort of things do you paint?"

"It's fairly abstract stuff really, most people have no idea what the painting is about, they just get a feeling from it."

"I think that sounds a good thing though, the painting will inspire a different feeling in each person, it makes the painting personal to them."

"I suppose it does, thanks for that, I never thought of it in that way before." Her smile is dazzling.

# BILL

I arrive at Leo and Gemma's home for some last-minute planning for winning Holly back. I'm so lucky my friends are willing to help me, I had been a total shit with them too, especially Adam. I had finally got my letter finished late last night, I just need advice now on when to send it to Holly. I can't decide whether to post it to her or give it to her at the party.

"Hey Bill, how's it going?" Leo greets me as he opens the door.

"I'm getting there, I think. I have a bit of hope left that I can make this right again." He steps back to welcome me into the house and I can hear female laughter coming from the kitchen.

As I walk into the kitchen though, the laughter stops abruptly and silence reins.

"Way to kill the mood mate." Adam laughs.

"Sorry, I know I'm about as popular as the plague at the moment."

"Oh, stop over exaggerating Bill, I'd say it's more like a fart in an elevator type of unpopular." Gemma snorts laughing at her own joke and just like that the atmosphere in the room lightens again.

"Bill, you have to stop beating yourself up now, enough, Holly won't be able to forgive you if you can't forgive yourself." Elissa touches my arm in sympathy.

"I wouldn't blame her if she couldn't."

"She can, trust us, she loves you and she understands why you reacted the way you did, you just need to give her a way to come back." Gemma is very serious now, all laughter gone from her face.

"Holly loves you Bill, she just doesn't feel like she has all of you, and she definitely doesn't feel like she has your trust, that's why she can't let herself answer any of your calls. She doesn't trust herself to be able to resist you, and she knows she deserves all the man she gives her whole heart to, she can't give her heart to a man who doesn't have a whole heart to give her in return." Elissa has tears in her eyes.

"God, I really fucked up, didn't I?"

"Well yeah, you did. Now put it right."

"You know Gemma? For a submissive you're an awfully bossy person." I smile at her.

"I'm giving her free rein at the moment, but not for much longer, soon she'll have to keep the bossy under control." Leo laughs.

"I thought that was your job Sir." Gemma winks at him.

"Don't push it too far sweetheart, you won't enjoy the consequences." His face becomes stern and I hear a small gasp from Gemma. Her cheeks flush and her eyes widen, someone is excited at the thought of punishment.

"Okay people, back to planning, Bill is only going to get one chance at this so let's make sure he doesn't mess it up again." Adam calls us all to attention.

"Thanks for the vote of confidence mate."

"Hey, I call it as I see it mate."

"So, Holly really thinks I'm not coming to the party?" I ask the girls.

"I told her you wouldn't be one of the guests at the party, which isn't technically a lie, but I still think she's going to be really mad at me." Elissa sounds worried.

"I told you, she'll be fine about it once she realises it was for her own good." Gemma gives Elissa a hug.

"I hope you're right."

There's a knock at the door and Gemma jumps up to answer it.

"Reinforcements have arrived." She exclaims as she walks past me.

I look at Leo confused, but he just shrugs his shoulder at me and shakes his head. I think he gave up trying to keep up with Gemma and her planning a long time ago. Discretion is the better part of valour after all, plus a good Dom knows when there's no point in trying.

I hear voices in the hall, one I recognise as Henry the other female voice I don't know.

They come into the kitchen and Elissa rushes to hug the young woman tightly.

"Bill, I'd like you to meet my Sister Sophie."

She turns her Sister around to introduce us. Sophie's eyes narrow at me and she doesn't look impressed at all.

"So, this is the infamous Bill then?" She looks me up and down.

"That's me."

"Well you don't look like a total idiot, I can only suppose you must have been under the influence of a total brain fart when you did what you did to Holly."

Well Sophie was a totally different person to her Sister, Elissa wouldn't say boo to a goose, and here this young thing was giving me a hard time.

"I am trying to put it right." I defend myself.

"Try Hard." She pokes me in the chest and I hear Leo, Adam and Henry sniggering behind me.

"How did you end up coming with Henry?" Elissa asks.

"We arrived at the gate at the exact same time." Henry answers.

"I can speak for myself you know." She turns and snaps at Henry.

"I never said you couldn't." He replies with a small smile.

She flushes with embarrassment and lowers her eyes. Well there's a surprise, feisty on the outside, submissive on the inside. I see Henry look at her with much more interest and Elissa turns to hide a small smile.

# HOLLY

The day of the party dawns bright and warm, inside I feel cold and grey though. I need to try and sort my mood out before I get to Elissa's cottage, I can't spoil today for her. At least I will look good, the dress Gemma persuaded me to buy, is so beautiful. A swirling soft brilliant red dress with thin spaghetti straps.

I shower and blow dry my hair, putting it up into a soft knot on top of my head, leaving a few tendrils brushing against my neck. I slip the dress on and look at the total effect in the mirror. The dress looks amazing, but I can see the dark circles under my eyes, I need more make up.

Once I've added some concealer and a slick of lipstick, I decide that's as good as it's ever going to get. I only need to stay long enough to congratulate the happy couple and share a couple of drinks, then I can come home and hide for a while.

The street outside Elissa's cottage is full of cars by the time I arrive, I can hear laughter and the swell of conversation coming from the garden at the back. I make my way around the side of the cottage towards the garden, just as Gemma turns the corner at the end of the house.

"Holly, finally! I was beginning to think you weren't coming." She reaches out and gives me a big hug.

"I said I was coming, didn't I." I hug her back.

"I know, but you really didn't want to." She laughs.

"I know, but you were right, this is Elissa and Adam's day and I should help them celebrate."

"I'm glad you're here, even if we had to guilt you into it." She smiles.

"It sounds like there are already lots of people here."

"Yes, lots of friends from the club, Henry is here and Sophie too."

"Oh Gemma, are you match making?" I laugh.

"Who me? Never." She says with a wink.

"Do you need me to help with drinks or food or anything?"

"No, we have special wait staff for today."

"I didn't know we were doing that." No one had mentioned that in the planning.

"There was a last-minute volunteer."

"Oh okay, well that's good then."

"I have something for you, now before you say anything, I want you to read it." She says firmly, pulling an envelope from her pocket.

"Gemma no, if it's from Bill I don't want it."

"You need to read it, even if it's just so you can move on." She says gently.

"Maybe, but today isn't the day."

"Just read it Holly, then you can relax and enjoy the party. Go and get a drink, then find a quiet spot on the beach and read it."

I take the envelope from her, surprised at its weight. There is more than a letter in there. Bill's firm bold handwriting spells my name across the front. I really don't want to read it, but Gemma is right, I do need to hear what Bill has to say.

## BILL

I take a deep breath and look around at all the guests, Holly still hasn't arrived, I'm not sure how she will react when she sees I'm here. I lift the tray of champagne flutes and do another circuit of the garden handing them out to guests.

This was part of my penance, not just to Holly, but to Adam too, I had punched him after all. I will be in service to the party until Holly sets me free, if she ever does.

Suddenly, there she is, coming around the side of the house with Gemma. She takes my breath away, she looks so beautiful. She has my letter in her hand, she looks around nervously at the guests. I see the exact moment she sees me; her whole body goes rigid and her face loses all its colour.

She turns and whispers furiously to Gemma, pointing in my direction. Gemma pins an innocent expression on her face and just shrugs. Holly stomps away towards Elissa and Adam, an angry look on her face.

I watch as she hugs Elissa and Adam kisses her on the cheek. I walk in her direction with my tray of drinks, time to push my little masochist a little bit.

"Drink miss?" I ask with a slight bow.

"Thank you……." Her words come to a halt when she sees it's me offering the drink.

Her hand is hovering over the tray, and she looks as though she can't decide whether to take one or not.

"Take the drink Holly." She grabs a glass automatically, then looks annoyed at herself for obeying my command.

She turns abruptly and walks across the garden towards the gate to the beach. I let her go, she has to come to me in her own time, hopefully my letter will help.

"Don't look so worried." Gemma says from behind me.

"I am worried, what if this doesn't work?"

"If it doesn't, it doesn't, but at least you will have tried. I have a feeling it will work though." She smiles.

"It has to work." I say firmly.

"Just relax and give her time."

"I'll try." I say as I walk away, looking down at the leather strap on my wrist, this has to work.

I move among the guests with my drinks tray, but I can't focus on any of the conversations around me. My whole focus is on the little spot of beach where Holly is, hopefully reading my letter. I keep glancing at the little gate, hoping to see her come back through it.

"Earth to Bill." Leo says laughing and waving his hand in front of my face.

"Sorry Leo, do you need a drink?"

"I would love a glass of wine, since you're offering."

"Well that is my job for the day after all." I offer up the half empty tray of glasses for him to choose from.

"You know the saying; A watched pot never boils." He takes a sip of his drink, laughter in his eyes.

"I know, but seriously, how log can it take to read a letter?"

"If she's read the letter, she will have a lot of thinking to do, a lot of decisions to make, that takes time, and you have to give her that time. You owe it to her."

"I do, it's just the waiting is killing me."

"It will be worth it when she is back in your arms."

# HOLLY

I can't believe he's here. Gemma and Elissa lied to me, tricked me into coming. They may have tried to wrap it up in a technicality by saying that they told me he wasn't on the list of invited guests, their excuse that he isn't actually a guest, but a member of bar staff, but that still makes it a trick in my book.

Now I am trapped on this beach with no escape except past him. I could just wait here until the party ends and everyone goes home, but that would be the coward's way out. I could read his blasted letter, I look down at the envelope still held tightly in my hand. What the heck could he have to say that he thinks will make it all okay?

There isn't anything that can make it all okay, I wish there was. My fingers move over the bulge in the envelope, what is it? My curiosity wins and I open the envelope to see what's inside. I tip up the envelope and a small pair of beautiful silver scissors fall out onto my hand.

Scissors! Why was the man sending me scissors? They are a beautiful pair, all engraved and ornate, like ceremonial scissors used to cut official ribbons. Taking a deep breath, I pull out his letter, the page is full.

I walk along the beach to a little post and sit down to read.

*Holly*

*I know sorry is a totally inadequate word for what I did that night, but I have to say it anyway. I also need to say sorry for what I didn't do. I didn't give you the trust I demanded from you.*

*I demanded that you give all of yourself to me, yet I was too cowardly to give you the same. You were far far braver than I was. I have been hiding a part of myself away from the world for too long. It was a self-preservation tactic.*

*Hannah ripped my heart to shreds and broke my trust in the world. I allowed her to keep a part of my heart, the part I should have given to you.*

*When I saw you in the corridor with Andrew my mind immediately shot back in time to the night I found Hannah with the other Dom. All my fears came back, and I couldn't see past them to see you were struggling with him.*

*When I walked away, I was running from the hurt of it happening again. The only way I could deal with it was to run away and hide. When Adam tried to stop me from leaving, I reacted without thinking and punched him, my own friend and I punched him.*

*I'm not proud of what I did and I'm not making any excuses, because there aren't any.*

*When we started our relationship, I told you there needed to be total trust and honesty between a Dom and his sub, but I didn't give that to you, I let you down in the worst way possible. I told you that you could rely on me, that I would deal with any problems you had. Then the first time you have a problem, I just walked away.*

*I can't even begin to imagine what you must have felt watching me walk away. You must hate me, although Gemma and Elissa keep telling me you still love me. The question is, can you ever forgive me?*

*I know there aren't enough words in the world to apologise to you.*

*The only words I offer now are the words from my heart. I love you Holly, and I can honestly tell you that I love you with the whole of my heart. I know that wasn't the case before, but I have claimed back the piece that Hannah kept. Today I give that piece to you, so that you now have my whole heart, I hold nothing back.*

*When I was helping you find yourself, I actually found a part of myself I thought had been lost forever. You gave me back my love of the scene, my inner sadist, my need to be close to someone. You gave me back my ability to love someone, you gave me your love and set mine free.*

*I hope with all my heart that you can forgive me.*

*Today I am in service to this party, and I will remain so until you release me from my duty. Around my wrist is a leather strap of service, I can't take it off, only you can do that. Use the scissors and set me free, forgive me and set me free, love me and set me free, and I will spend the rest of my life showing you exactly how much I love you.*

*Love with all my heart*

*Bill.*

Tears are running down my face as I read the last lines of his letter. The honesty of his words and the love he talks about, the fact that he would show his own vulnerability in such a way is stunning.

The fact that he would put himself in service, in front of all his friends, people who have known him as Dominant for so long is shocking. I look at the scissors in my hand, he has given me the ability to set him free.

Can I forgive him though? I love him, that's true, but what he did hurt so much. I know why he did it, even before he confirmed it in his letter, that doesn't make it any easier to take though. The words he wrote to me are so beautiful, full of love, he had never expressed himself like this before. I had never really expected him to, men don't normally.

He has laid his heart bare on the page, could I do the same again though? What if he let me down again? I don't think I would survive this again. Can I trust his words? He had told me I could rely on him before, then he let me down.

So many thoughts and questions are chasing each other around in my head, circling and swirling until I almost feel dizzy. I need to get back to the party, and I need time to think.

# BILL

She's been on the beach for a long time, I want to go to her, but I know I have to wait for her to come to me. It has to be her choice, her decision, just as it is in the D/s side of the relationship. I can't put any pressure on her now.

Finally, I see her at the little gate, she's been crying, I put tears in her eyes again. She looks around until her gaze lands on me, her eyes lock with mine and I see her breath catch. She looks at me and her bottom lip quivers, then she turns away and walks over to Gemma and Elissa.

They both lean over and give her big hugs and Elissa offers a tissue. Holly dabs at her eyes and blows her nose, then she takes a deep breath and pulls her shoulders back. She is so strong, so brave. I watch as she mingles with the other guests, a smile on her face, but I can see the tightness to her smile, she might be putting a brave face on things, but she isn't happy.

"You're going to bore a hole in her back if you keep looking at her like that." A female voice says behind me.

I turn to see Elissa's little sister, Sophie standing with a big smile on her face.

"Would you like a drink?" I hold out my tray.

"No, I've had quite enough already thank you."

"Are you enjoying the party?"

"I am, Elissa looks so happy, blissful and beautiful." She sighs wistfully.

"Do you have a man in your life?"

"No, I've been far too busy with studying and working to bother with men."

"Well that does take up a lot of time, but now you've finished your degree you should get out and live a little."

"That's the plan, I intend to let my hair down for a while." She says with determination.

"Good plan."

"So, do you think Holly will forgive you?"

"I hope so, that's all I can do, hope."

"I think she will, you just needed to show her how sorry you are."

"Well hopefully I have done, we'll just have to wait and see. Now if you'll excuse me, I have drinks to serve."

I look around to find Holly again, there she is, sat with her friends, all three of them chatting away. They suddenly all burst into laughter at something Gemma has said. My God she is so beautiful, I rub my chest to ease the stab of pain, I really can't lose her, this can't be the end.

Suddenly she glances in my direction and gives me a small tentative smile. My heart jumps into my throat, that is the first positive feeling I've got from her since that night at the club. Maybe she was finally softening to me a little.

Just as suddenly the smile disappears, and she looks away sadly. I turn and collect fresh drinks from the bar area and walk over to the pretty pergola to see if anyone needs a full glass. Everyone is enjoying the party, I have seen lots of club members mingled in with Adams staff and old ladies from the village, along with a little dog who seems to keep escaping from its owner.

Everyone is mingling with everyone else. This is the beauty of our lifestyle, no judgement, no scorn. We are all free to do what we need.

I just need Holly to come to me now. Then my life will be complete and I will be able to hold the woman I love.

## HOLLY

I have felt his eyes on me all afternoon, like the heat from the sun the heat from his gaze warms me deep inside. The silver scissors feel heavy in the pocket of my dress, should I use them and set him free? If I do that, he will definitely think I have forgiven him, and I'm not sure I can do that.

I look out over the garden from my seat at the top of the waterfall, Gemma, Elissa and I are sitting on the rocks at the top of the hill.

"This garden really is beautiful Elissa." I sigh.

"It is, Adam made it perfect for me." She beams at me.

"You are so lucky."

"I am, Adam loves me with all his heart." Her smile is beautiful.

"So how are you feeling now Holly? Did you read Bills letter?" Gemma asks.

"I read it yes, and I don't know how I feel. I do still love him, but how can I trust that he will be there for me when I need him?"

"He's so sorry for what he did, he loves you."

"He probably does, yes, but that's not enough."

"Don't decide anything too quickly Holly, take your time and think about it fully." Elissa says.

"You're right I know, but I can't leave him waiting for too long, that would just be cruel."

"Well then, give yourself a deadline, the end of the party, then you make your decision." Gemma says firmly.

"That's a good idea. Thank you, ladies, for being there for me, for caring." I squeeze both their hands.

"You are our friend, of course we will be there for you."

"Well, no one ever has been before." I laugh.

"You have us now, you aren't alone."

"Thank you, now, I really must nip to the loo, too much wine."

I jump up quickly, so they don't see my silly tears, and head down the slope towards the house.

Once I've used the loo, I wash my hands and repair the damage to my face from all the tears. When I look sort of respectable again, I make my way out of the house back into the garden.

As I walk along the path towards the seat at the end, I bump into someone coming the other way.

"Oh, I'm so sorry." I say, but my words die in my throat when I see who it is I've bumped into. Andrew!

"You will be sorry when I'm done with you." He snarls.

"What are you doing here? You aren't supposed to come anywhere near me." I cry.

"You need to pay for what you did to me." He grabs my arm and pulls me around the side of the cottage, away from the view of everyone at the party.

"I didn't do anything to you, you were the one who attacked me."

"You led me on, you little bitch, then you ruined my life. I've been fired, I'm going to end up with a criminal record, how am I going to get another job now." His grip tightens on my arm and I wince in pain.

I feel sick, no one is going to see us here, he could do anything and no one will know.

"Let me go Andrew, don't do anything stupid. Just let me go, let me go and leave." I plead.

"I don't think so, you need to pay, you little tease."

He pushes me against the wall and my head bangs painfully against the brick.

## BILL

Looking round I realise I can't see Holly. Elissa and Gemma are still sitting at the top of the waterfall, but Holly isn't with them any longer. I can't see her anywhere, I walk to the little gate and look down the beach to see if she is there, but it is deserted.

Has she left without giving me an answer? I didn't think she would just leave, maybe I should have spoken to her instead of waiting. She would have said goodbye to Elissa and Gemma though, even if she didn't want to speak to me.

I walk up to where the girls are sitting chatting.

"Have you seen Holly?"

"She went to the bathroom, why?" Gemma asks with a giggle. I think someone has had a bit too much wine.

"How long has she been gone?" I snap.

"What's wrong Bill?" Elissa asks.

"I don't know, I can't see her anywhere. Has she been gone long?"

"She has been a while, about twenty minutes actually." She frowns.

"Do you think she went home?"

"No, she would have said bye, she just said she was nipping to the loo." Gemma looks worried now too.

"She could be on the beach, I know I always find it a good place to think things through."

"No, I've checked, the beach is empty."

I turn and scan the guests again, looking for a glimpse of her red dress. Nothing! She isn't there.

I rush down the hill and head into the house to see if she's still inside. I don't know why I have such a bad feeling, but I really need to find her.

There are a couple of people hanging around in the kitchen.

"Has anyone seen Holly? Blonde, wearing a red dress?"

"Yes, she went outside a few minutes ago, I think she walked left."

I rush back out of the door and along the path to the corner of the cottage. The sight that greets me when I turn the corner freezes my heart. Holly is backed up against the wall by a man, they are pressed together like lovers.

Then I hear her pleading with him.

"Andrew please let me go, don't do anything stupid, let me go."

Fucking hell, what the fuck is he doing here? How is he even out of jail?

"I'd suggest you do as the lady says you bastard."

Both their heads snap around to look at me.

"Fuck off Bill, walk away like you did last time." Andrew snarls at me.

Holly gasps and tears pour down her cheeks.

"I don't think so, now let her go."

"I don't think I'm ready to do that just yet." He laughs.

Holly looks at me with pleading eyes full of fear. I try to reassure her with my smile, but she just shakes her head and more tears fall.

She doesn't believe I'm going to help her, she thinks I'm going to walk away again.

I walk closer to them, until I'm only a step or two away, I wait until he looks at Holly again and then strike. I grab the back of his shirt and yank him so hard he falls backwards and lands on his arse in the dirt.

Holly sags against the wall, as though her legs won't hold her weight anymore.

"Holly, get behind me. NOW!" I yell when she is too stunned to move.

She peals herself away from the wall and staggers behind me, just as Andrew gets up from the floor. He steps towards me and I can smell the alcohol on his breath.

"That bitch ruined my life, she needs to pay." He shouts.

"She didn't do anything Andrew, you fucked up your own life, and you're only making it worse now by breaking the restraining order. The police will be called and you'll be arrested again."

"Fuck you!" He shouts and lunges for me.

I'm sober though and he has had more than enough alcohol, my fist meets his jaw before he's even got close. His head jolts back and his eyes roll back in his head. He stays upright for a few seconds, a stunned look on his face, then he goes down again. Flat on his back on the floor, out cold.

I hear Holly sob behind me and turn to pull her into my arms. She resists for a few second, then with a huge gulping sob, she collapses against my chest.

"It's okay girly, it's all over, you're safe now."

I look over her shoulder to see Leo coming around the corner.

"What the hell?" he says looking at Andrew unconscious on the floor.

"Leo phone for the police, will you?"

"Of course mate, where did he come from?"

"The pub, by the smell of him." I rub Hollys back gently.

Leo pulls out his phone and makes a call to the police.

"They're on their way."

"Good, do you think we can get away without anyone at the party noticing? I really don't want this to spoil Adam and Elissa's day."

"Too late mate, here they come now."

I turn to see Adam, Elissa and Gemma, followed by several guests coming from the garden to see what's going on.

"You found her then?" Gemma says.

"Just in time I think." I point at Andrew still out cold on the floor.

"What the hell is he doing here?" She walks up to Andrews prone form on the drive.

She looks down her nose at him in disgust, then quite deliberately kicks him in the balls.

"Oh dear, I seem to have accidentally stepped on a worm." With a flick of her hair she walks back to Leo and into his arms.

"Well done sweetheart." Leo kisses her hard.

"Is Holly okay?" Elissa asks from the comfort of Adams arms.

"She will be." I pull Holly tighter against my chest.

"I'm glad you didn't punch me that hard." Adam laughs.

"I trust the police are on the way to clear this mess off my driveway?" Elissa asks.

"Yes, I called them, they're on the way." Leo confirms, just as we hear the sound of sirens coming down the road.

# HOLLY

I can hear police sirens, and I bury my head further into Bills shoulder in embarrassment. I've totally ruined Elissa and Adams party, caused a scene again.

How did Andrew even know where I was? I suppose with so many members of the club here, it wouldn't have been too hard for him to find out. Why do this though, surely, he's just made it worse for himself, especially with so many witnesses. Anger doesn't make people think straight though I suppose.

I shudder at the memory of his hands on me again, and Bill rubs his warm hands across my shoulders and down my back. He pulls me in tighter and I feel warm and safe again, like coming home. Then I remember we aren't together anymore. He had walked away last time. Not this time though, this time he had stayed, had stood between me and danger.

The police car pulls onto the drive and two officers get out. One of them is the officer who took my statement after the incident at the club.

"Okay, who wants to tell me what's going on here?"

"It's simple officer, there is a restraining order against this man coming anywhere near Holly, he decided to ignore it and gate crash a private party to attack her again." Bill explains.

"I see, are you okay Miss? Are you hurt or injured in any way?"

"I'll probably have bruises on my arms where he grabbed me and I banged my head on the side of the house when he pushed me against it, apart from that though I'm physically okay yes."

Emotionally is another matter though, I can't understand why he had become so fixated on me, he was a good-looking man, he could have found someone who wanted to be with him.

"What happened to him?" The police officer asks as Andrew begins to come around, groaning and clutching his crotch.

"He lunged at me and I defended myself by punching him once." Bill admits.

"You punched him in the balls?" The officer looks as though he's trying not to laugh.

"No, I punched him on the jaw."

"Then why is he in pain in the trouser area?"

"That could be because I didn't see the mess on the floor and accidentally stepped on it." Gemma says, an innocent expression on her face.

The other officer helps Andrew sit up, and he shakes his head as if to clear the fog. He looks around and then his eyes lock on me and Bill.

"I want that man arrested for assault. He knocked me out." He shouts.

"From what the witnesses say, it was self-defence and he only punched you once. You however have now attacked this woman twice, this time breaking a restraining order put in place after the last time. Paul arrest him for breach of his bail conditions and breaking the restraining order. Do you wish to press charges for this assault Miss?" He turns to me.

"I just want him to go away, that's all I want, for this to be over." I sob.

The officer called Paul begins to read Andrew his rights and places him in hand cuffs, Andrew starts protesting again.

"I'm the one that was punched here pal, I was knocked out, and what the hell happened to my balls?"

He's still shouting and screaming as they load him into the police car. Most of the guests have drifted back into the garden, leaving only a few people behind.

"You will both need to come into the police station to make a statement, but I don't see any need to trouble you with that today, try and enjoy the rest of your party and we'll be in touch."

He gets into the police car and drives away.

"Well that's the drama over with, lets get back to enjoying the party shall we." Leo says, trying to lighten the mood.

Taking a deep breath, I pull away from Bill.

"I just need a few minutes alone." I say and turn to walk into the house.

"You shouldn't be alone just now Holly." Bill says, concern in his voice.

"I do perfectly fine alone Bill, I've been doing it most of my life now." I snap, I need to get somewhere by myself before I totally fall apart.

## BILL

I watch as she walks away from me and disappears around the corner of the cottage. My chest actually hurts and for a few seconds I can't seem to get enough air.

"Hurst doesn't it?" Gemma whispers in my ear.

"What does?"

"Watching the person you love with all your heart walk away from you. Now you really know how she felt that night." She says with satisfaction.

I gasp as the realisation sinks in, I had known that I had hurt her, but I really hadn't realised what it felt like. It feels like she has ripped my heart out of my chest and left it on the floor.

"Just give her a few minutes to get herself together, she's had a big shock." Elissa, as usual is sympathetic.

"Plus, it gives you some time to decide what you are going to do with your new awareness of what you did." Gemma slaps me on the shoulder.

I look at the leather strap on my wrist, will she ever cut it off?

"Don't give up hope yet, hang on till the end." Leo says.

"Well, it seems that's all I can do."

"It's going to be okay you know."

"I'm sorry all this spoiled your day Adam, you too Elissa."

"Every party needs a bit of excitement." Adam laughs.

We all walk back to join the party, all of us a little subdued. I decide to do a circuit with more drinks, try to get the party back on track.

As I move through the guests with my tray of drinks, naturally the main topic of conversation is the commotion on the drive way. Most people are saying how awful it is that Holly had to deal with any of this, some are shocked by Andrews behaviour, not everyone had heard about the incident in the club, and like most people, had thought that Andrew was a decent guy.

It just goes to show how wrong you can be about people.

My attention keeps returning to the open back door of the cottage, watching for Holly coming back out. After twenty minutes there's still no sign of her though. Do I go in and find her? Do I send Gemma in to check on her?

I don't know what to do anymore. I'm so scared of doing the wrong thing, so worried that the wrong thing might be doing nothing.

## HOLLY

My mind was a swirling mess of thoughts, all fighting to be heard. Confusing, contradictory thoughts. Bill had stayed this time, had kept me safe, but he knew now that there was nothing going on with Andrew. What if something happened with someone else? Would he trust me then? Or would he assume the worst?

I want to believe that he trusts me totally, but I'm so scared of being hurt again. Maybe it would just be easier to be on my own, less exciting, but so much easier.

Then I remember how it had felt to be held securely in his arms, how safe and protected I felt. The thought of never feeling that again takes my breath.

So many questions, so few answers, it feels like my brain might explode along with my heart. I try to relax and let go of the questions, clear my mind of all the clutter, hoping that the right answer will be the only thing left.

I lose track of how long I've been sitting on the stairs, my mind drifting away. Suddenly one conclusion comes into sharp focus in my mind. It's so simple I can't understand how I didn't find it sooner.

Either I love him enough to forgive him, or I don't.

So simple, yet it really is the only question I need to answer.

I jump up from the step and rush down the stairs. Of course I love him, I never stopped loving him. Surely we can work everything else out if we love each other.

I feel the weight of the scissors in my pocket, and I know what I need to do. I need to set him free.

I rush out of the door into the garden, but I can't see Bill anywhere. I look around frantically, but he isn't in the garden. Oh God, did I wait too long, did he give up and leave?

Tears rush to my eyes, how can it be too late?

"Holly? Are you okay?" Sophie asks, putting her arm around my shoulders.

"Did he leave already? Did Bill leave?"

"No Holly, he didn't leave, he went down to the beach, I think he wanted to be alone." Henry says coming up behind Sophie.

Thank goodness, I still have time. I rush to the gate and down onto the beach, kicking my shoes off on the way to make it easier to walk on the sand.

There he is, further down the beach looking out at the sea. He looks so alone and so sad, my heart aches. I run along the beach, shouting his name as I get closer to him.

He turns to see who's calling his name, and his face fills with hope as he sees it's me. I almost bump into him I'm rushing so much.

"Is everything okay Holly?" He asks concerned.

"Yes Sir everything is wonderful." I beam at him.

His face fills with dawning hope.

"Are you saying what I think you're saying?" He grips my elbows tightly.

The sun glints off the scissors as I reach for his wrist, I cut through the leather strap and lift his hand to kiss the inside of his wrist.

"I set you free Sir, free to live, free to love, free to be happy. I love you Sir."

"Thank God." He exclaims pulling me into his arms and kissing me deeply.

When he pulls away, we are both gasping for breath and a bit flushed.

"I love you Holly, I am so sorry that I didn't protect you, more than that though, that I actually hurt you even more. It was only when you walked away from me earlier that I truly realised how much I did hurt you."

"You protected me today." I stroke his cheek with my hand.

"I should have done that last time, without question. I failed you."

"Well, you'll just have to spend all your time making it up to me, won't you?" I say with a cheeky grin.

"Watch it girly, try and remember who is in charge here." He gives me his sternest Dom face and yanks my head back with my hair.

"I love you Sir." I whisper.

"I love you too Holly." He says, then kisses me so gently I have tears on my cheeks when he pulls away.

I rest my head against his chest and just enjoy the feeling of being held by the man I love, who happens to love me back.

THE END

Printed in Great Britain
by Amazon